Virginia Vineyards

FORBIDDEN LOVE

USA TODAY BESTSELLING AUTHOR

ASHLEY FARLEY

CHAPTER 1
DANIEL

Daniel takes in the surrounding landscape. The backdrop is worthy of a portrait with rows of grapevines stretching deep into the valley and the late-summer sun descending beyond the mountains. He experiences a pang of jealousy. Although he'll never admit it to anyone, the view from Foxtail Farm's cafe terrace beats the one from his own vineyard next door. He may be getting on in his years, but his expansion plans are far from being complete. He aims to make Love-Struck not only the most magnificent vineyard in Virginia but on the East Coast.

The bride is stunning in a strapless satin gown, her groom a dapper figure in a slate-blue suit. Placing her back to her audience, she tosses the bouquet over her head, which then whirls through the air toward the women clustered in front of Daniel. Among this group are his daughters, Ada and Casey, and his mistress of ten years, Ruthie. When the bouquet lands in Casey's hands, she lets out a shriek and drops it like a hot potato.

"I don't want it!" she cries, staring down at the bouquet as one might a snake. "Luke and I have only been dating a few weeks." She tugs on Ada's arm. "You should have it, since you're already engaged."

Ada swats Casey's hand away. "No thanks! Enzo and I have agreed to a long engagement."

Scooping up the bouquet, Ruthie presses the flowers to her nose and bats her eyelashes at Daniel. He gives his head a slight shake, and she pokes her lower lip out in a pout.

"The flowers are gorgeous. I'm keeping it despite what you think," she says in a low voice meant only for him.

Daniel glances around to see if his daughters are watching them. Thankfully, they are distracted by the band who has retaken the stage. He waits until Ada and Casey wander off with their significant others before he says, "What was that about, Ruthie? I hope you're not going to start harassing me about marrying you."

She moves in close to him. "Why not, Daniel? We're not getting any younger, and I don't want to grow old alone."

"You know how I feel. Marriage ruins relationships," he says, his voice a low hiss.

"Not always. Plenty of couples are happily married. I understand you're gun-shy after your troubled first marriage. But you and Lila were incompatible. You and I have been blissfully cohabitating for ten years." Ruthie's eyes shine with unshed tears. "If I didn't know better, I'd think you're embarrassed to be seen with me."

"You know that's not true." The lie slips easily from his tongue. Daniel's peers would laugh him off the planet if he married a blonde bombshell diner owner.

She removes a tissue from her handbag and blots her eyes. "Then why do we have to keep our relationship a secret?"

"You know why," Daniel snaps.

"Because you don't think I'm good enough for you. And you're waiting for someone better to come along."

Daniel scowls. "This conversation is getting old."

The band slows its tempo from an old R&B tune to a country love ballad. Ruthie grabs Daniel's hand and tugs on his arm. "Dance with me. Let's go public with our relationship. You'll see. Our friends and families will be happy for us."

Daniel jerks his hand free. "Stop it, Ruthie! You're embarrassing yourself."

"Fine!" Ruthie brings herself to her full height, thrusting out her voluptuous breasts and holding her shoulders back. "I'm going home. And don't bother coming over later. Your whore is taking the night off." Her bleached blonde updo bounces around on top of her head as she teeters off in spiked heels.

Daniel experiences a fleeting sense of loss as he watches her disappear into the throng of wedding guests. Why is she going rogue on him now? She's never expressed dissatisfaction with their arrangement before. Is it possible their relationship has run its course? He loves Ruthie, just not enough to marry her.

The lead singer announces the cutting of the cake, and Daniel migrates with the crowd to the cake table at the edge of the terrace. The bride and groom, each with a hand on the knife, slice into the cake. During the cake feeding process, which Daniel has always found silly, he eavesdrops on the surrounding conversations.

"They make a handsome couple," says a pretty brunette in front of him.

Her friend hums her agreement. "Ollie is drop-dead gorgeous."

The brunette places her hand over her heart. "Imagine how adorable their child will be with Sheldon's wavy blond hair and Ollie's aqua eyes."

The friend shakes her head as though in wonder. "I can't believe she's pregnant. She certainly doesn't look it."

"She's not very far along," says the brunette. "I bet she'll be one of those annoying women who barely gains any weight."

Daniel's emotions are conflicted about his youngest son's marriage to the intriguing young vintner from California. He's thrilled Sheldon finally found the love of his life, but he worries Ollie will coerce Sheldon into leaving Love-Struck to work with her at Foxtail.

Once they're finished with the cake, the bride and groom

return to the dance floor, where they pass out neon aviator sunglasses and light-up sticks to the guests. The band kicks into full swing, playing songs that remind Daniel of late-night fraternity parties in college.

The sight of Ada dancing in Bud's arms is like a knife to Daniel's heart. Daniel raised Ada from birth. She was his daughter, his pride and joy, until several months ago when they discovered Bud is Ada's biological father. Daniel's stomach churns when he thinks about his friend and his wife having an affair under his nose.

Ada is the picture of elegance in a shimmery gold evening gown with her dark hair twisted into a knot at the nape of her slender neck. Daniel has often dreamed of walking Ada down the aisle at her wedding. He and Ada have talked about this special day from the time she was a child playing dress-up in princess costumes. Now that she's engaged to her Italian prince, that day will soon be coming.

A thought occurs to Daniel that sends a sharp pain to his gut. Bud has the means to give Ada a lavish wedding. Bud will have the honor of walking her down the aisle. And Daniel can't let that happen. The problem is, Ada is furious at Daniel for the way he's treated her these past few months. And Daniel doesn't blame her. He's been a real jackass. He made the terrible mistake of believing Ada could no longer be his daughter because she doesn't carry his DNA. Daniel has much to atone for. And there's no time like the present.

Daniel makes his way toward them on the dance floor. Tapping Bud on the shoulder, he asks, "May I cut in?"

"That's up to Ada," Bud says, looking down at his daughter.

She levels a steely gaze on Daniel. "No, thanks."

"Please, Ada. Just one dance." When Daniel tries to take hold of her arm, Bud shoves him away.

"You heard her, Daniel. She doesn't want to dance with you. Now buzz off."

Daniel goes after Bud with fists flying, landing a solid punch to his left eye socket. Daniel's oldest sons, Hugh and Charles, pounce on him and drag him off the dance floor.

Hugh grips Daniel's arm to steady him. "What's wrong with you, Dad? Why would you cause a scene at Sheldon's wedding?"

Daniel looks from Hugh to Charles, who appears as though he might cry. Daniel raised his four children to set high expectations for themselves and to strive for perfection. He also taught them to be strong, to face adversity head-on, and to go after their enemies with a vengeance. Hugh has hung on his every word, while Charles has never paid him any attention. And it shows. Hugh is ruthless and Charles spineless.

Daniel jerks his arm free of Hugh's grasp. "I'm sorry. I let Bud and Ada get the best of me."

Hugh narrows his eyes. "I don't understand. You kicked Ada out of the family. And now you're suddenly upset she found her biological father?"

Daniel hangs his head. "I'm not suddenly anything. I've been torn up about this situation from the beginning. But my emotions were misguided. I directed my anger at your mother onto Ada."

"But Mom's been dead thirteen years," Charles mutters.

Daniel glares at his son. "I'm aware, son. But that doesn't make her affair with my oldest friend any less painful."

Hugh chimes in, "You're no saint either, Dad. You were having an affair with Casey's mother at the same time."

Daniel throws up his hands. "Don't remind me! Beverly screwed me, too. She hid my biological daughter from me in New York while I was down here in Virginia, raising another man's daughter as my own. Can you blame me for being angry?"

With eyes lowered, Charles says, "I agree it's a messed-up situation, but you've gotta let it go. Ada is Bud's daughter now. You were cruel to her. You drove her away. And you only have yourself to blame."

Hugh and Daniel stare at Charles with mouths agape. He rarely contributes to a conversation, personal or business related.

Daniel slaps Charles on the back. "You're right, son. I made a colossal mess of things, and now it's my responsibility to fix them."

CHAPTER 2
LANEY

Laney stares in disbelief at the scene unfolding on the dance floor. Her father-in-law is a notorious bully, but she's never known him to hit anyone. When Hugh and Charles drag Daniel to a remote corner of the terrace, Laney imagines the conversation as she watches the men with their heads pressed together. Hugh will undoubtedly be reading his father the riot act. She knows his wrath well. She's experienced it many times.

When the threesome part ways, Hugh strides angrily toward her. "Come on. We're going home." He brushes past her and walks fifty feet before realizing she isn't following him. He motions for her to come with him, but she shakes her head.

He closes the distance between them. "I'm tired, Laney. Today, I played thirty-six holes of golf. I'm ready to go home."

"That's your problem. Sheldon is your brother, Hugh. We should stay until the bride and groom leave."

"Fine! You can stay. But I'm leaving, and I'm taking the girls with me. They're bored out of their minds." He stomps off toward their twelve- and thirteen-year-old daughters, Ella and Grace, who have been sitting alone at a table, staring at their phones, for most of the evening.

Laney waits until her family has left the reception before slipping her feet out of her heels and grabbing a pair of cheap flip-flops from the wicker box beside the dance floor. She makes her way through the crowd to the stage where she parties with the band as though she were back in college.

Hours later, she reclaims her shoes and drifts with the other guests to the front of the cafe to see the newlyweds off. Her periwinkle silk dress clings to her sweaty body, and her damp hair hangs in curtains around her face, but she hasn't felt this alive in years.

She lines up with the others, waiting with fistfuls of rose petals for the bride and groom to appear.

"Were you a carrot top as a child?" says a voice beside her, loud enough to be heard over the din of laughter and chatter.

Laney is surprised to see Love-Struck's new winemaker standing next to her. Bruce wears his ginger coloring well. They look enough alike to be siblings with the same deep auburn hair and smattering of freckles across their noses. She would kill for his emerald eyes. While she finds her gray-blue hue pretty, her eyes are too small and close together.

Laney giggles. "Like Little Orphan Annie minus the curls. What about you?"

"My hair was as orange as Ronald McDonald's. I'm Bruce Wheeler. We met at my welcome reception. I'm having trouble keeping all the members of the Love family straight. If I remember correctly, you're married to either Charles or Hugh."

Laney smiles. "Good memory. I'm Laney Love, Hugh's wife."

Bruce's emerald eyes dart about as he scans the crowd. "Where is Hugh? I caught a glimpse of him earlier in the evening."

"He went home a while ago. He was tired after playing thirty-six holes of golf." This last tidbit of information is unnecessary and catty. But she's tired of making excuses for her husband's absence at important events.

Something resembling disapproval crosses Bruce's face. Hugh

should be here. Sheldon is his brother. "I'm headed back to town soon if you need a ride home," Bruce says.

"Thanks, but I have my car. I came early to arrange the flowers for the ceremony."

"Cool! So, you're a florist?"

"Not in the traditional sense. I don't own a floral design shop. I assist a woman who arranges flowers for local weddings. Since Sheldon is my brother-in-law, Ollie asked me to do her flowers. This was my first solo performance."

Bruce appears impressed. "I know little about flowers, but the arbor at the ceremony was outstanding. Were those roses?"

Laney bobs her head. "All grown in the garden at Love-Struck." She snickers. "I picked the bushes clean early this morning. There isn't a single bloom left."

"I wasn't aware of a rose garden. Where at the vineyard is it located?"

"Behind the main house. Rumor has it Hugh's mother was quite the gardener. When I first discovered it, the bushes were in pitiful shape. I've nursed them back to health, even adding a few new varieties every year."

"So, you're not only a floral designer, you're a gardener as well."

Laney smiles. "In my book, the two go hand in hand." Over the crowd, she spots the top of Sheldon's golden head. "Look! Here they come now."

The bride and groom, still dressed in wedding attire, emerge from the cafe and make their way through the tunnel of people to an antique convertible Cadillac. Sheldon helps Ollie into the back seat, climbs in after her, and the car speeds off down the driveway with a trail of tin cans clattering behind them.

"Where are they going on their honeymoon?" Bruce asks as he walks Laney to her car.

"To the Homestead for a few days. But Ollie doesn't want to be gone from the vineyard for too long."

Bruce smiles. "I admire her drive."

When they reach her Suburban, Laney unlocks the doors and turns toward him. "I enjoyed chatting with you, Bruce. I'm at Love-Struck a lot on the weekends, arranging flowers for weddings. I hope I see you around."

He leans over and kisses her cheek. "I hope so too. Drive safely."

Laney floats home on a cloud. She can't remember the last time she had so much fun or made a new friend.

Letting herself in the front door, she hums an old Motown tune as she makes her way to the back of the house for a glass of ice water. When she enters the dark kitchen, her husband's booming voice startles her.

"Where have you been?" Hugh emerges from the darkness, tumbler of whiskey in hand.

Laney's happy bubble bursts, and she deflates back to reality. "You know where I was, Hugh. At your brother's wedding."

Hugh lifts a strand of stringy hair off her shoulder. "Then why is your hair all messed up?" He leans in close, sniffing. "And you stink. Why have you been sweating?"

Laney retrieves a tumbler from the cabinet. "I was partying with the band," she says, jamming the tumbler into the ice dispenser on the refrigerator.

Hugh's breath is hot on the back of her neck as she fills the tumbler with water. "I don't believe you. You were singing when you came in. I haven't heard you sing in years. Tell me who you were with? I want to know if you're cheating on me."

She spins around to face him. "I'd sing more often if you gave me a reason to."

"I would, if you weren't such a cold-hearted bitch."

Laney rolls her eyes. "Here we go again with the insults. If that's what you really think of me, why won't you divorce me?"

"Because I don't want a divorce. I want a wife who welcomes me into her bed."

"Then let's see a therapist," Laney says in a pleading tone.

"With counseling, we might rekindle some of the passion we once shared."

"You know how I feel about shrinks, and I'm not giving you a divorce. You're welcome to leave any time you want," he says, sweeping an arm toward the front door. "But I'm keeping the house and the girls, and I'm not giving you a red cent."

"Then we'll continue to live in misery," Laney says, and drags herself up the stairs to the guest room where she's been sleeping for more than a year. The thought of him touching her body makes her skin crawl. Truth be told, Laney and Hugh are far beyond counseling. There is nothing left of their marriage to save.

When they met in college, Laney, an unsophisticated farm girl from Arkansas, had been impressed by Hugh's family's wealth—their fancy cars and sprawling estate—she'd overlooked his foul moods and unpleasant demeanor. She'd put up with the bullying, thinking he'd mellow once they had children. By the time their second child was born, Laney knew their marriage was in trouble.

Ella and Grace are acutely aware of their parents' marital problems. Laney has heard them whispering late at night. The vicious arguments scare them, and they find the uncertainty about their future unsettling. The girls are aware of what's coming. Some of their friends' parents are divorced. They want to know who they'll live with, and if they'll have to move out of the only home they've ever known.

The situation is toxic for all of them. If only Laney could figure a way out. She doesn't come from money like Hugh. If he makes good on his threats, she could lose everything. She's amassed a small savings from the money she's earned arranging flowers. One of Ella's friend's moms is the best divorce attorney in town. But there's no way Laney can afford her fees. She could hire a cut-rate lawyer, but Hugh's team of high-powered attorneys would devour that lawyer's lunch.

Laney has grown accustomed to her lifestyle. She doesn't want to give up her beautiful home on Willow Lane, one of the town's most desirable streets. But she can't live like this much longer. She needs to think of something soon.

Laney brushes her teeth, washes her face, and changes into her pajamas. And like she does every night at bedtime, she drops to her knees beside the bed and prays to God to give her courage to move on with her life as a single mother.

CHAPTER 3
ADA

Ada arrives at the equestrian center before dawn on Sunday for a sunrise trail ride with her father. Bud is tacking up his chestnut Arabian, Phoenix, when she enters the stable. He looks up from cinching his saddle. "Morning, sunshine," he says with a wide smile.

"Oh, my gosh!" Dropping her purse on the ground, Ada rushes over to him and cups his face in her hands. "Your eye is literally black. This is all my fault. I'm so sorry."

Bud draws her hands away from his cheeks, bringing them to his lips. "You have nothing to be sorry for. And it's definitely not your fault. After what happened, I don't blame Daniel for being sore at me." His blue eyes sparkle with mischief. "Don't you think the bruise makes me a manly man?"

She laughs out loud. "Indeed, I do."

He lets go of her hands. "We need to get a move on if we want to see the sunrise. You gather your tack, and I'll get Glory out of her stall."

They work together to groom and tack up Ada's dapple-gray thoroughbred. When they emerge from the stable fifteen minutes later, the sky has lightened. Mounting their horses, they pick up a trot as they cross the pasture to the trail's entrance, making it to their special spot as the sun is creeping over the mountains.

Sliding down off their horses, they stroll over to a large boulder. Bud removes a thermos of coffee from his backpack and fills two disposable cups. Sitting down on the boulder, they watch in silence as the sky transitions from mauve to a buttery yellow.

"I have a proposition for you," Bud says, finally. "I want you to work for me part-time at the equestrian center. The hours are flexible. I think it'll dovetail nicely with your wine shop venture."

Ada furrows her dark brow. "What would I be doing? I'm too qualified for mucking out stalls."

Bud laughs. "Not as a stable hand. As my assistant. I'll be grooming you to one day take over Malone Equestrian Center."

"Bud, no! I appreciate your generosity, but I can't accept. When the time comes, Stuart should have the property."

"Stuart has no interest in horses. He'll sell the business before the ink is dry on my death certificate. I've helped him a gracious plenty in the past. I financed his wealth management firm and gave him a significant down payment on his house. Besides, he'll inherit other assets. I've given this considerable thought. I want you to have the farm, which includes the stable, house, and surrounding acres. You can argue all you want, but I've already changed my will."

"Do we have to talk about this?" She rests her head on his shoulder. "I just discovered you're my father. I hope you're not planning to die on me anytime soon."

"I'm perfectly healthy. But I'm not getting any younger, and I am slowing down some. I would appreciate having someone share the responsibilities."

She wraps an arm around his neck. "And I would love working here with you. But I don't want to cause any more friction between you and your son. I was hoping Stuart would've come around by now."

"He's being stubborn, but he'll come around, eventually. I'm not worried about Stuart. My relationship with my son is solid.

You are my priority right now. We have a lot of making up to do. Working together on the farm is a great way to do that."

"I'm flattered, and I would love to accept your offer. But I should check with Enzo first."

"Of course! As your fiancé and business partner, he needs to be onboard. Take all the time you need to make this decision. I'm not just offering you a job. I'm asking you to make a commitment to the future."

"You're the best, Bud." She kisses his cheek. "I'm grateful to have you in my life. And I'm sorry again about the black eye."

Bud chuckles as he gives her face a loving pat. "No worries. I'll take a punch for you any day."

Ada drains the last of her coffee. "I admit, I found Daniel's behavior last night odd. Why the change of heart? He's been a jerk to me for months and suddenly he wants to dance with me?"

"I'm sure he misses you. He probably realized what an ass he's been and wants to make amends. He's loved you like a father all your life. Try as he might, he can't just turn that off."

"Maybe not. But I resent him toying with my emotions. My relationship with him is over."

———

Ada finds Enzo in his kitchen making blueberry pancakes. She's spent every night here since they got engaged nearly a month ago. She misses her sleek apartment with its all-white furnishings and contemporary art collection. But not enough to sacrifice being with Enzo. She hates pouring rent money down the drain, but Enzo has yet to invite her to move in with him.

He glances up at her as he transfers pancakes from the griddle to two plates. "You're glowing. Did you meet up with some handsome stranger on your sunrise trail ride?"

She hooks an arm around his waist from behind and kisses his neck. "You're the only handsome man for me."

He sets down his spatula and turns to face her. "Then why the rosy cheeks?"

"Fresh air and exciting news. Bud asked me to work part-time for him to prepare me for taking over the equestrian center one day. He's leaving the equestrian center to me when he dies. Obviously, I hope that is decades away, but his offer touched me deeply."

Enzo grins. "You're a perfect fit for the job. What did you tell him?"

"That I needed to talk to you."

He kisses the tip of her nose. "Then let's do that while we eat. Before our pancakes get cold."

Enzo adds slices of bacon to the plates while she pours two glasses of orange juice. Gathering napkins and flatware, they take their breakfast outside to the umbrellaed table on the terrace.

Ada pours maple syrup over her pancakes. "Bud has already changed his will. The equestrian center will one day be mine, whether I decide to work for him now." She forks off a bite of pancakes. "It's a dream come true, even though I never identified it as a dream. Does that sound weird?"

"Not at all." Enzo stuffs a whole slice of bacon into his mouth at once. "Opportunities turn into dreams all the time. I never considered becoming a sommelier until I was waiting tables and became interested in wine."

"And now, not only are you a certified sommelier but you're opening your own wine shop." Ada pauses a beat. "The question is, Can I handle two jobs at once? I think I can, since they will both be part-time. But what if it turns out to be too much?"

"Then we'll make adjustments. We can easily hire someone to oversee the cheese business."

They discuss the pros and cons of Ada accepting Bud's offer while they eat. When they finish, they take their plates to the kitchen and return to the terrace with steaming mugs of coffee. They settle into lounge chairs and tilt their faces to the late-morning sun.

"You realize you haven't slept in your apartment since we got engaged." Enzo cracks an eyelid as a smirk tugs at his lips.

Ada sits up in her chair. "Are you getting tired of me already?"

"On the contrary. Your lease is up at the end of September. I'm suggesting you move in with me."

Ada settles back down in her chair. "I've thought about it, actually. I like knowing my apartment is there if I need my space."

"Which you haven't in the past month," Enzo says.

"True. But I can't see myself living in your masculine show house of testosterone."

Enzo barks out a laugh. "Anymore than I want to live in your powderpuff apartment. I guess we'll have to buy a new house and merge our tastes when we get married."

"Speaking of getting married . . . I've been thinking—"

"That we shouldn't wait two years?" He grabs her hand. "Say the word, and I'll marry you tomorrow."

Ada sips her coffee. "When you asked me to marry you, waiting a couple of years seemed like the proper thing to do. Now it feels like time wasted when we could be building our lives together. Look at Sheldon and Ollie. They've only been together a short time. They were on a speedy path to the altar before she got pregnant."

Enzo rolls onto his side to face her. "My feelings for you won't change. You're my soul mate, Ada. If anything, my love for you grows more every day."

She smiles softly at him. "And mine for you."

Enzo pulls out his phone and thumb-types on the screen. "I've been monitoring the local real estate market. There's a house coming on the market a couple of blocks away." He jumps up and pulls her to her feet. "Let's walk over and look at it."

"You mean, now?" she says, looking down at her riding britches and boots.

"Yes, now. It's a short walk," he says, dragging her inside.

Passing through the house, they deposit their coffee mugs in the kitchen before heading out the front door and walking down the street in the direction opposite Magnolia Avenue, the town's main thoroughfare. The early September sun is hot, and sweat is soon trickling down her back. But the change of seasons is upon them, and autumn is Ada's favorite time of year.

Enzo takes hold of her hand. "Have you given any thought to what kind of wedding you want?"

"I've always dreamed of getting married in the chapel at Love-Struck. The whole town would be in attendance to watch Daniel walk me down the aisle. As a child, I used to hide out there to escape my parents' arguments. After Mom died, I spent long hours kneeling at the altar and praying for her return. I still go there sometimes. I feel closest to her in that chapel."

"What about the reception?" Enzo says in a soft voice.

A faraway expression crosses Ada's face. "It would be over the top with sailcloth tents on the lawn in front of the winery. We'd have exotic flowers and gourmet foods flown in from all over the world. A funk band would entertain our guests until a helicopter whisks my new husband and me away to a private plane waiting to take us to the South of France for a month-long honeymoon."

Enzo cocks an eyebrow at her. "That's quite the extravagant affair."

Ada kicks at a rock on the road. "Just another dream down the drain, like so many others."

"Who says you have to give up this dream? Bud has a nice spread of land. Why can't you have the wedding you described at his place?"

Ada shakes her head. "Our relationship is too new. It wouldn't be right. Maybe in a year." She leans into him as they stroll. "All the more reason for us to wait."

"We could always have a small wedding, as in just the two of us at some romantic destination in the Caribbean."

She play-smacks his arm. "What kind of wedding is that? I want the white dress. I'm not passing up the opportunity to be a princess for a day."

"What's a single day mean when you're going to be a princess for life?"

"Will any of your family travel from Italy for the wedding?"

Enzo shrugs. "I'll invite them, but I doubt they'll come. My guest list will be short. I haven't lived here long, and I only know a few people in town. Even more reason to elope," he says with a devilish grin.

Ada laughs. "I draw the line at elopement, Enzo."

He hunches a shoulder. "Can't blame a guy for trying."

They arrive at the for-sale house, ending their discussion of weddings. "How is this house any different from yours?" she says about the charming taupe-colored bungalow. "Why don't we redecorate yours to accommodate both our tastes?"

"My house is already bursting at the seams. No way your furniture will fit. We need to buy something we can grow into." He pulls out his phone and reads the details of the listing. "This one has three bedrooms, but approximately the same square footage. Oh, well. We can cross this one off the list." He pockets the phone, and they turn back toward home.

Ada recognizes his disappointment. "If you really have your heart set on buying a bigger house, we might as well look in earnest."

His face brightens. "I'll reach out to my Realtor. He can start sending us listings as they come on the market."

"What will we do if we find something we like? Contribute equal equity with both our names on the title instead of Mr. and Mrs.?"

"All the more reason for us to elope." He stops walking and turns to her. "It would certainly simplify our lives."

"Especially considering my messy family situation. Let me think about it."

She can see how much this means to Enzo, and she doesn't want to disappoint him. But Ada plans to marry only once, and he's the love of her life. She wants her wedding day to be special.

CHAPTER 4
DANIEL

D aniel watches Ruthie crack two eggs into a skillet sizzling with butter. No one can make eggs sunny-side up like she can. And her made-from-scratch blueberry muffins are out of this world.

She pretended to be angry when he showed up last night, but Daniel could tell she was happy to see him. She's as reliable as an old hound dog. To his relief, she took his side when he confessed to starting a fight with Bud.

She may be unsophisticated and uneducated, but she's a damn good listener. And damn good in bed too. Several years ago, he bought her this small Victorian house—prime Lovely real estate on the corner of Jasmine and Grapevine Avenues. In exchange, she allows him to come over whenever the mood strikes. Daniel thinks of the pink house as his safe place. He can be himself here.

Ruthie removes the eggs from the pan and adds two sausage links, a scoop of grits, and a blueberry muffin to the plate. She sets the plate on the table in front of him and sits down across from him with her coffee.

"Everyone in town is talking about the Coleman girl's wedding next weekend," she says, her eagle eyes peering at him over the brim of her mug as she sips.

Daniel shovels grits into his mouth and groans in pleasure. "Biggest wedding we've ever hosted. We're expecting close to six hundred guests. Our new event planner doesn't have the experience of handling such a lavish affair. With Ada gone, I've had to enlist Casey's department to help with the arrangements." He gulps down some freshly squeezed orange juice. "I'm capping all future wedding receptions at six hundred. This wedding business is getting out of control. We're a vineyard, first and foremost." He complains, but the weddings bring in considerable income.

"Sounds like great fun to me. I assume you're invited," Ruthie says, shredding a paper napkin, a nervous habit that grates Daniel's nerves.

"Of course, I'm going. I've known Jack Coleman all my life." He eyes the napkin, and her hands go still.

"Take me as your plus-one, Daniel. This would be the perfect opportunity for us to go public with our relationship."

Daniel sets down his fork and wipes his mouth. "We've been together for ten years, Ruthie. Why are you rocking the boat now?"

"I told you last night. I want a man to spend my golden years with. Not just on the occasional Saturday night when you can take time off for me from your busy social schedule. Is that so wrong?"

"I wouldn't call it wrong. It's just not realistic," Daniels says, and returns his attention to his breakfast.

"I'm not getting any younger. I've worked hard all my life, and I'd like to enjoy myself while I still have my health. I'm thinking of selling the diner. This town is growing at such a rapid rate, I imagine I'll get a pretty penny for it." Ruthie gets up and parades around the room, her slinky robe flowing behind her. "I want to travel and spend long days being pampered in a luxury spa. I may plant a vegetable garden and take art classes."

"Nobody's preventing you from doing all that."

She stops walking and stares at him with mouth agape. "You're not listening to me, Daniel. I don't want to be alone."

Daniel bites down on a sausage link. "Then we have a problem, because I'm not getting married."

"And I'm solving the problem by ending this relationship." Ruthie stomps out of the room, returning seconds later with an empty cardboard box. She drops the box on the floor beside him. "Pack your stuff. I want you out of my house."

"It's not your house. I bought it for you, remember?"

Ruthie plants a hand on her curvy hip. "Doesn't matter. My name is on the deed."

Daniel stands to face her. "You didn't seriously think I'd let you keep the house."

"I'll sue you, or better yet, I'll tell the world about our affair." She removes her phone from her robe pocket and waves it at him. "I have Beth Matthews on speed dial. She's a regular at the diner and a journalist for the *Lovely Gazette*. I'm sure she'd be interested in hearing the story of Daniel Love's secret mistress."

Daniel jerks his head back as though she slapped him. "Are you blackmailing me?"

"Pretty much." She kicks the empty box with the toe of her velour bedroom shoe. "Now pack your stuff and get out of my house."

"Let me at least finish my breakfast," he says, plopping back down in his chair.

Letting out a guttural growl, she grabs the plate, walks it across the kitchen, and drops it in the sink with a loud clatter.

"Geez. There's no need to be so hostile."

"Hostile is mild compared to the tantrum I will throw if you don't get the hell out of my house. Now move it." Grabbing him by the arm, she hoists him to his feet and marches him up the stairs to her bedroom.

Ruthie hovers over him while he packs his few belongings in the box—reading glasses, toiletries, pajamas, and some random articles of clothing. With arms folded over chest, she scrutinizes his every move as he dresses in tennis whites.

"Stop with the prison guard act. I'm not going to steal anything. Believe me, you have nothing I want."

"I'm making sure you don't forget anything. I don't want you to have an excuse to come back. I never want to see you again."

Daniel looks down his nose at her. "You just chased off your best customer."

"I'm sure the diner will survive. My clientele will be better off without you."

"Whatever. Truth be told, I'm glad this relationship is over. You've become quite the bore." Picking up his box, he hurries down the stairs and out the back door to the garage, where he parks his car so the neighbors won't see.

Overwhelming sorrow envelops him as he drives down Grapevine Avenue toward the center of town. His life will be less fulfilled without Ruthie in it. But he refuses to be bullied into marriage. When she cools off in a few days, she'll come begging for him to forgive her.

Daniel drives straight to the country club for his weekly doubles match with his three closest friends. But he plays badly. His heart isn't into tennis today. His mind is on Ruthie. What if she doesn't come crawling back to him?

He showers in the locker room, but instead of having lunch on the terrace with his friends, he heads toward home where he can be alone with his thoughts. Parking in front of his stone mansion, known to locals as The Nest, he sets out on a walk around the grounds.

He crosses the lawn to the winery building. Administration offices occupy the second floor with tasting room and cafe on the first. There's a line waiting for a seat at the tasting bars, and every table in the cafe is occupied. He can't postpone his renovation plans any longer. His goal is to move the tasting room to the nearby barrel building and turn the lunch cafe into a proper bistro, offering dinner hours. He'll knock out the back wall and install sliding glass doors opening onto a much-needed terrace.

Excitement floods him, and he makes a mental note to schedule an appointment with his architect for next week.

When he returns to the house, he finds Casey lounging by the pool.

"Hey there!" She smiles up at him from a romance novel. "What're you up to?"

"I just got home from playing tennis at the club. Mind if I join you?" Without waiting for her response, he stretches out on the chaise lounge next to her.

Casey closes her novel. "This is my last Sunday here. I'm moving into my condo on Wednesday."

Daniel's heart sinks. He's losing another special someone. "Is it that time already?"

"Can you believe it? The month passed quickly. Tonight might be our last dinner together. Next week will be busy with moving and preparing for the Coleman wedding."

Daniel will miss their dinners. Now he'll be dining alone. "Let's make tonight a going away party. We can invite Sheldon."

"Sheldon and Ollie are on their honeymoon, remember?"

His smile fades at the mention of Ollie. He can no longer invite Sheldon to dinner without including his new wife. Will Daniel ever get any alone time with his son?

Casey's fingers graze his arm. "Are you okay, Daniel? You seem sad."

Daniel considers opening up about Ruthie to Casey. But she came into his life only a few months ago, and he doesn't know her well enough to confide his deepest secrets.

"I'm sad because you're leaving. I hope you won't be a stranger. You're welcome here anytime. You don't even have to call first."

"Don't worry. I'll definitely be using you for your pool," she says with a charming giggle.

Daniel shields his eyes from the sun as he looks over at her. "How's the furniture shopping going?"

"Slow," she says. "Everything is so expensive and poorly

made. I took your suggestion and looked around in the attic. I saw a couple of things I'd like to have, but I wanted to check with you first."

"Take anything you want." Daniel forces a smile. He's terrible company and needs to be alone. He throws his legs over the side of the chaise lounge. "I'm going to change into my swimsuit. I'll be back in a few."

Hurrying up to his room, he sits down on the edge of the bed and stares at his phone. He longs to call Ada, to talk to her about Ruthie. Ada has been his confidante since she was old enough to understand grown-up problems. She never casts judgement, and she almost always has a solution. Often an unscrupulous one. He smiles to himself, thinking about some of her warped schemes.

Of all his children, Ada is the most like him. They are both self-centered and vindictive, and determined to have their way no matter who gets hurt. How ironic that she's not his biological child.

The image of Bud and Ada dancing last night at the wedding reception comes to mind. A beautiful daughter and her handsome father. Her *biological* daddy. But Daniel is her father too. He nursed her bee stings, rocked her back to sleep when she woke from nightmares, and took her to Europe to celebrate her sixteenth birthday.

A wave of anger sends him to his feet. He wants Ada back. And he shouldn't have to share her with Bud. He needs to figure out a way to turn Ada against Bud. Or Bud against Ada. He paces the room as he strategizes. And he knows just where to go for help.

He taps on Bud's son's contact information and thumbs off a text. *I have an urgent personal matter to discuss with you. Do you have time for lunch tomorrow?*

CHAPTER 5
LANEY

On Monday morning, Laney sees her daughters off on the school bus and heads out for a walk. She's two blocks from home when a dark gray Cadillac Escalade pulls up beside her. The passenger window rolls down and Sylvia calls out, "Hey there, hon. I've been trying to reach you. Do you have the list of flowers we need to order for the Coleman wedding this weekend?"

Laney steps over to the open window. "I finished it this morning. I can text it to you when I get home."

Sylvia presses her ruby-red lips thin. "I need it now. I'm leaving soon for Charlottesville. My daughter and her husband are going to a medical conference in Arizona, and I am taking care of the grandchildren. I'd like to place the order before I go."

Irritation crawls across Laney's skin. Sylvia's domineering personality is growing tiresome. Laney does all the work while Sylvia waddles around barking orders. If she didn't enjoy floral design so much, she would have quit a long time ago. "Why don't I just place the order for you?"

"Fine." Sylvia retrieves her purse from the passenger seat and digs around for her phone. She taps a manicured fingernail on the screen, and seconds later, Laney's phone pings in the pocket of her running shorts. "I sent you the contact information, including the address, for the wholesale florist in Hope Springs. I won't be home from Charlottesville until noon on Saturday. You'll need to pick the flowers up early that morning and drive them to Love-Struck."

Laney's irritation morphs into anger. "Seriously, Sylvia? This is the biggest wedding we've ever done, and you're expecting me to do all the work. I can handle it this time. But I have a family to take care of, and my girls are busy on the weekends. You need to give me more advance notice the next time you go out of town."

"Watch your tone, missy. I can always find another helper if you aren't up for the job." Sylvia rolls up the window and speeds away.

Laney stares with slacken jaw at the Escalade's retreating taillights. *A helper? Is that all I am to you, Sylvia?*

Laney's blood reaches its boiling point. She's tired of everyone bullying her. She's not a runner, but today she needs to blow off steam. She jogs for three miles without stopping to catch her breath, and by the time she reaches the center of town, she's calmed down.

Laney strolls down Magnolia Avenue, pausing to window-shop at her favorite boutiques. She's entering Ruthie's Diner for her morning cup of joe when she notices a sign in the store's window next door, announcing it available For Sale or Lease.

At the back counter, Ruthie fills a to-go cup with black coffee and hands it to Laney. "Would you like a muffin to go with that? Cranberry orange is the flavor du jour."

"That sounds delicious. May I please have it in a bag to take home?" Laney slides her credit card across the counter. "I noticed the building next door is available. What business was there before? Was it a dry cleaners or one of those mail room services?"

"Alterations," Ruthie says as she processes the credit card charge. "A Korean woman, Min Yung, owned the business. And good riddance to her. She came in here for lunch nearly every single day. And she always found something to complain about."

Ruthie's disgruntled tone surprises Laney. The diner owner is always pleasant and never has a bad word to say about anyone. She looks more closely at Ruthie. Behind her pink-framed reading glasses, her eyes are swollen as though she's been crying.

"Are you okay, Ruthie? You don't seem like yourself."

Ruthie waves away her concern. "I'm fine. I've just got some stuff on my mind. Are you doing the flowers for the wedding this weekend? I understand it's gonna be a humdinger."

Laney chuckles. "Humdinger is right. I'm worried we've bitten off more than we can chew," she says and leaves the diner with her coffee and muffin bag.

She pauses on the sidewalk out front to admire the building next door. The brick facade is painted taupe and a green awning covers the large windows on either side of the black front door. Moving closer to the building, she peeks in the window at the barren space inside—hardwood floors, drab walls, and a utilitarian checkout counter.

To her knowledge, there has never been a florist in Lovely. Even Delilah's Delights, the gourmet grocery on the side of the building opposite the diner, doesn't sell flowers. With a little fixing up, the storefront would be an ideal spot for a floral shop.

The sign says For Sale or Lease by Owner. She certainly can't afford to buy the building, but she might be able to lease the storefront. Laney snaps a pic of the contact information before heading home. She walks slowly, sipping her coffee as she considers the possibilities. Why is she working for Sylvia when she's capable of doing it all herself?

At home, she sits down at her small desk in the kitchen and places the flower order to the wholesale florist in Hope Springs for a Saturday morning pickup. She opens her laptop and spends hours reading best practices for starting your own business and shopping for display racks, refrigerator equipment, and worktables. She's so engrossed in her research, she doesn't hear Hugh enter the house at lunchtime.

He comes to stand behind her, looming over her as he stares at her computer. "I don't have much time, Laney. Can you fix my lunch? You can shop online later."

Laney slams her laptop shut and jumps to her feet. "I wasn't shopping. I was paying bills, and I lost track of time."

He takes in her exercise clothes and messy ponytail. "Why haven't you showered yet today?"

"I told you, I got sidetracked." She brushes past him on the way to the refrigerator. "I have some leftover rotisserie chicken. Do you want a salad?"

"Never mind. You go up and shower. You smell like rotten eggs. I'll make a sandwich and take it back to the office."

Laney glares at him. "You should try sweating sometime. If you exercised regularly, you could lose that spare tire around your stomach," she says, and hurries upstairs to her room.

Closing and locking the door, she sits down on the edge of the bed with her cell phone. Taking a deep breath, she punches in the number for the building's owner. She's surprised when a woman answers.

"Hello, this is Laney Love calling about the storefront for lease on Magnolia Avenue."

"Nice to hear from you, Laney. I'm Diana Gladstone. Are you interested in a tour?"

"Yes, please! Can I see it today?"

Diana chuckles. "I admire your enthusiasm. Unfortunately, I'm out of town and won't be back until midweek. Would late afternoon on Wednesday work? Say around five o'clock?"

"Wednesday at five is perfect. I'll see you then."

Laney falls back on the bed and stares up at the ceiling. The thought of starting her own business scares her to death. But it might be the answer to her prayers. Having financial independence is the first step toward divorcing her husband.

———

Laney is waiting on the sidewalk in front of the building when Diana Gladstone arrives. She appears younger in person than she sounded on the phone. She's mid-sixtyish and attractive, with a slim figure, mahogany shoulder-length bob, and clear green eyes.

Laney holds her hand. "Nice to meet you, Diana. Our town is so small, I thought I'd met everyone. But you don't look familiar."

"Lovely is my second home," Diana explains. "My primary residence is in Richmond. My husband recently passed away from a sudden heart attack. His career was commercial real estate. This is one of many properties I'm dealing with. The building is for sale if you're interested."

Laney shields her eyes from the sun as she lifts her gaze. "What's upstairs?"

"A furnished apartment with a living room and kitchen combo on the second floor and two bedrooms on the third. My husband recently renovated the kitchen and baths. He was thinking of renting through Airbnb. Since the town has become a popular wedding destination, he thought parents of the brides and grooms might appreciate the larger space an apartment offers over a hotel room."

"That makes sense. Is it available now on Airbnb?"

"Not yet. Honestly, I'd rather find a buyer for the building."

"Have you had much interest?"

Diana shakes her head, the clean edges of her bob skimming her shoulders. "I'm surprised, considering how fast the town is growing."

Laney tries to imagine living here. A two-bedroom apartment on Magnolia Avenue is a far cry from her spacious home on Willow Lane. The girls would have to share a bedroom and walk to the nearest bus stop. But Laney would have her freedom, and the three of them could live in peace.

"Shall we?" Diana says, holding the door open for Laney.

Laney enters the drab showroom. "Would you mind if I painted?"

"Mind? I would be grateful. The space could use sprucing up. What kind of business are you in?"

"I'm a floral designer. I do mostly weddings now, but I'm hoping to expand."

A sad smile spreads across Diana's lips. "My husband would approve. He was always bringing me flowers. He often complained there was nowhere in town to buy a quality bouquet."

"He was right. We're long overdue a florist." Laney gestures at the swinging door behind the counter. "May I?"

"Of course," Diana says and follows her into the back. "There's a small office and a restroom and lots of open space for you to create fabulous flower arrangements."

Laney sticks her head in the office and bathroom. "I would need to install a commercial grade sink and walk-in refrigeration. I understand these units are custom made and easily removable."

"That wouldn't be a problem. A plumber could tap into the existing water supply."

"And what are the lease terms?"

"Five years," Diana says and tells her the amount of the monthly rent.

Laney works hard to keep a straight face. The rent is more than she expected, but not out of the realm of possibility. "I'm just beginning the process of starting my business. I'll have to get loan approval in order to purchase the equipment."

"I understand." Diana opens the back door to show Laney the alley. "As you can see, there's ample room for you to park your car plus a delivery van."

Laney hasn't thought about a delivery van. Her Suburban will have to do for now.

Diana closes and locks the door. "There are many Loves in town. Which branch of the family do you belong to?" She says this with an air of nonchalance, but Laney knows she's fishing for information. She wants to know why Laney needs a bank loan when she's a member of the prosperous Love family.

"The Love-Struck Vineyard side of the family. Hugh is my husband." Laney hesitates, deciding how much to say. But her intuition tells her she can trust Diana. "He would back me if I asked. But I'd rather do this venture on my own."

Diana's face softens. "Good for you. I hope you can make it work. I'll let you know if anyone else expresses interest."

Laney brightens. "Thank you! That would be great!" She circles the back room once more before returning to the showroom.

At the front door, Diana says, "Coincidentally, I may sell my home if you know anyone who might be interested. It's a small farm just outside of town."

"A farm? What do you grow?"

Diana laughs. "Mostly corn. My late husband was a hunter. We pay a farmer to harvest the field. The view is lovely, and there's a small stream that runs through the property. I hate to leave the area, but I'm considering moving to Montana to be near my son and his family."

"I can't think of anyone off the top of my head. But I'll keep it in mind. Thank you for your time, Diana. I'll be in touch soon," Laney says, waving over her shoulder as she hurries down the sidewalk.

Tingles of excitement flutter in her belly as she walks home. She's taken the first step toward building a new life for herself and her girls.

CHAPTER 6
ADA

Ada and Enzo look at houses until her head spins. All different styles and sizes and locations. How can so many houses be on the market at once? It's as though everyone in town is taking part in a game of musical houses.

"There are things I like about each house," Ada tells Jamie, the Realtor. "But I'm not in love with any of them."

"That's part of the process," Jamie says. "You are determining what features are most important."

Ada aims a finger gun at him. "Exactly. Our perfect house would have the screened porch from Maple Avenue, and the Cape Cod's outstanding master suite, and the yard with the fabulous view and sunken fire pit." She scrunches her brow. "Which house was that? I've forgotten."

"The farm outside of town," Enzo says, tugging on her ponytail.

Jamie chuckles. "It's no wonder you're confused. We've seen a lot this week, and I know you're overwhelmed. But I wanted you to be aware of everything currently on the market. I've scheduled an appointment to see a new listing for early tomorrow morning. It's more than you want to spend, but it's worth looking."

"What's the point if we can't afford it?" Ada asks.

Jamie and Enzo exchange a look Ada can't interpret. "Jamie shared the MLS listing with me. This one is special, Ada. I don't see any harm in having a tour."

"If you say so," Ada says in a skeptical tone.

Touring a house they can't afford is a waste of everyone's time. And she's more than a little irritated when she falls in love at first sight. The contemporary home is all windows and sharp edges and built into the side of the mountain.

"This is insane, Enzo. We can't afford this."

"Maybe not, but I'm curious to see it," Enzo says, and gets out of his pickup truck before she can argue.

Ada traipses along beside him. "This is a bad idea. I already love this place. Are you torturing me for a reason?"

Enzo puts his finger to his lips, silencing her as he rings the doorbell. Jamie lets them in and shows them the house, which was built five years ago and features a chef's kitchen, marble baths, and a family room with an enormous stone fireplace. A bluestone patio with a built-in fire pit makes up the top level of the terraced yard with an infinity pool on the level below, both offering stunning views of the mountains.

Ada throws up her hands in surrender. "That's it. I'm done. I'll never find another house I love as much as this. I'm so mad at you two for bringing me here."

"Will you give us a minute alone?" Enzo says to Jamie.

"Sure thing. I'll be in the kitchen if you have questions," Jamie says, and retreats inside the house.

Enzo turns to her. "I can afford the house, Ada."

Ada lowers herself to the bench surrounding the fire pit. "So, you've been holding out on me. Is there no end to your supply of royal money?"

A smirk appears on his lips. "There's an end. We're just not anywhere near it yet."

She folds her arms over her chest. "But I want to contribute. Otherwise, it won't feel like my house."

Enzo sits down beside her. "If that's what you really want," he says, fingering her cheek.

Ada grabs his hand, pulling it away from her face. "We're not married yet. What if we break up?"

"That's never going to happen. But if it makes you feel better, we'll have an attorney draw up an agreement. Better yet, we can elope."

Ada grunts. "I already told you, we're not eloping."

Enzo pulls her close, kissing the top of her head. "We're getting ahead of ourselves, babe. Jamie tells me there are several motivated buyers. We have to submit the winning bid first."

She pushes away from him, sitting up straight. "Then let's do it. We'll make a no-contingency offer with as big a down payment as we can manage. I don't like to lose, Enzo."

"I'm aware. And I have no intention of losing."

———

Ada leaves Enzo and Jamie to work out the details of the contract and heads over to Malone Equestrian Center for an arranged meeting with Bud. Reclaimed pine paneling lines the walls of his study and sunlight beams in through french doors that lead to a wrap-around porch. Bud hands her a file and they sit side by side on a leather-upholstered love seat.

Bud settles back and crosses his long legs. "I thought I'd start by giving you a broad overview of my operation."

A gentle breeze drifts through the open doors, and Ada's mind soon wanders. *What will happen when I inherit the equestrian center? For the safety of the horses, I should live on the premises. But it'll break my heart to sell the contemporary house. Then again, Bud's Lowcountry-style home is much larger, with at least four bedrooms for all the children I plan to have.*

Bud taps her on the shoulder, breaking her reverie. "Earth to Ada. You're a million miles away."

Ada's face warms. "I'm sorry. I'm not usually so distracted. Enzo and I are making an offer on a house today."

Bud closes the file in his lap. "That's exciting. Tell me about it."

Ada shows her crossed fingers. "Not until we get it. I don't want to jinx us."

Bud chuckles. "I understand." He takes her folder and gets to his feet. "The first hint of autumn is in the air today. Why don't we walk the property? I can tell you more about the business as we go."

"Good idea. Maybe the crisp air will clear my mind and help me focus," Ada says and follows him out the french doors and across the porch.

As they stroll toward the stable, Bud says, "Does this mean you and Enzo will live together? I don't mean to pry. And I certainly don't mind. Cohabitating prior to marriage is the norm with kids these days."

She smiles. "We're pretty much living together now, honestly. We're thinking of moving the wedding up."

They pause at the outdoor arena to watch a group riding lesson in progress. "I'd like to host your wedding, Ada, either here or at the country club. I would be honored if you'd allow me to give you away."

A vision pops into Ada's mind. She's stunning in a Carolina Herrera gown on the arm of her distinguished, tuxedo-clad father. Only the father in her imagination is Daniel. "That's incredibly generous of you, Bud. But we haven't decided what kind of wedding we want. We may even have a destination wedding. I'll definitely keep you in the loop."

"I'm happy for you, Ada. Life is good." He leans on the railing, a broad smile on his lips.

"You seem extra chipper today. Did something happen?"

"I finally convinced Ruthie to go on a date with me. She's agreed to be my plus-one for the Coleman wedding."

Ada's golden-brown eyes go wide. "You mean Ruthie from the diner?"

Bud laughs. "She's the only Ruthie I know. I've been trying to get her to go out with me for years."

Ada squeezes his arm. "Go, Bud! She's a beauty. And loaded with personality."

"She's a looker, all right. Unfortunately, I think she's more interested in attending the wedding than dating me. I'll show her a good time, and we'll see where it leads us."

She leans into him. "You don't give yourself enough credit. You're quite the catch. Any woman would be lucky to get a man like you."

"Having you around is good for my ego." Bud pushes off the railing. "Let's keep moving. I want to be mindful of your time on such an important day."

Bud spends the next two hours giving her a bird's-eye view of his operation. When he receives an important phone call, he excuses himself and returns to his study to take it.

Ada is unlocking her car door when Stuart appears from nowhere, grabbing her by the arm and spinning her around to face him. "You thieving little bitch. I'm not gonna let you get away with it."

"Get away with what?" Ada says, wrenching her arm free of his grasp.

"Stealing my inheritance. This farm belongs to me."

Particles of Stuart's spit ping her face, and she runs the back of her hand across her cheek. "But you don't even like horses."

"Who cares? I plan to sell the farm, the whole kit and caboodle. The property is worth a fortune."

Ada waves a hand in the direction of the house. "Talk to your father. It's his estate. I have nothing to do with it."

"Like hell you don't. You can disclaim your inheritance."

"How can I disclaim it when I haven't inherited anything yet?"

"You know what I mean, Ada. Tell Dad you don't want the farm. Tell him it's rightfully mine." Stuart's menacing tone sends chill bumps across her skin.

Ada pins him with a death glare. "And if I don't?"

He grabs her arm again, squeezing it hard. "I'll make your life a living hell."

It was not so long ago when Ada said this same thing to Casey. And she made good on her threat. She slashed Casey's tires and ransacked her house. The anger consumed her. Ada understands all too well how it feels to have a half sibling suddenly invade one's life. "I was hoping you and I could have a relationship. Can we at least try?"

"No thanks. I never wanted a sibling when I was a child, and I certainly don't want one now."

Ada swallows the nasty comeback on the tip of her tongue. "I'm sorry you feel that way." She pries his fingers from her arm, shoves him out of the way, and gets in her car.

As she's driving off, Stuart shouts, "Disclaim your inheritance, Ada. Or you'll regret it."

She's still shaken from her encounter with Stuart when she stops at Delilah's Delights for take-out lunch. She focuses on picking out salads without paying any attention to the other customers. While standing in line to pay, she hears a familiar voice behind her say, "Hello, Ada."

She glances over her shoulder. "Hi, Da . . ." She stops herself from calling him *Dad*. She gives him a curt nod. "Daniel."

"I'm glad I ran into you. There's an empty table on the deck out back. Do you have time to eat lunch with me? I have something important I want to talk to you about."

Curiosity gets the best of her. "I can spare a few minutes, but I'm going to wait and eat with Enzo."

They finish paying and go outside to the deck. Ada sets her shopping bag of salads on the table. "Enzo is waiting for me. I don't have much time. What did you want to talk to me about?"

"As you know, I'm not good at admitting when I'm wrong. But I'm ashamed of the way I've treated you." Daniel stares down at his unopened salad container. "Anger has consumed me these past few months. I'm furious at your mother for cheating on me with my oldest friend and at Bud for sleeping with my wife. I was heartsick to learn the precious little girl I raised as my daughter is not my flesh and blood. For unjustified reasons, I pushed you away. But I miss you so much, and I want you back in my life."

His words touch Ada. She realizes how difficult it was for him to say these things. But they can't change the past. "I'm sorry, Daniel, but we can't go back to the way things were before Casey entered our lives."

His pale olive eyes are full of genuine sorrow. "Maybe not, but we can forge a new relationship built on the close bond we once shared. Can you at least try to forgive me?"

"Even if I'm able to forgive you one day, I'll never be able to trust you again. And you can't have a relationship without trust."

Tears sting Ada's eyes as she leaves, knowing their close bond is gone forever. While she's devastated by that loss, she's felt more at ease, more herself, these past months. She's no longer under pressure to live up to his high expectations. Bud and Enzo accept her for who she is despite her many flaws. She must tread lightly where Daniel is concerned. If she gives him an inch, he will take a mile. And she refuses to be his puppet ever again. He is now Casey's problem.

CHAPTER 7
LANEY

Laney spends the early morning hours on Friday cutting greens from her yard and the extensive gardens around Love-Struck. When she's finished, she parks behind the barrel building and unloads the buckets from the back of her Suburban. She's filling the buckets with water when it suddenly dawns on her. If she divorces Hugh, she'll no longer be able to take advantage of the vineyard's grounds and facilities. Her life will be less comfortable and convenient. She'll be excluded from family festivities at Love-Struck—Easter brunches and Thanksgiving dinners. She'll be forced to share the girls with Hugh on the holidays, which will make for lonely times for Laney. Living on a strict budget, she'll have to cut coupons for groceries and buy less expensive skin care products. This seems like a high price to pay for her freedom.

She's so caught up with her concerns, she doesn't hear Bruce approach until he's looming over her. "What's all this?"

Laney straightens, one hand on her aching lower back. "Greenery to go with the flowers for tomorrow's wedding."

Bruce chuckles. "Did you leave any greenery on the bushes?"

"Ha ha. I left plenty." She opens the door to the barrel building's cool storage room and begins dragging the buckets inside.

"Can I help you?" Bruce asks, following her into the storage room.

She eyes his business attire—blue and white windowpane shirt and khaki pants. "Thanks for offering, but I'd hate for you to mess up your clothes. You can hold the door open for me, though."

"Sure thing!" He leans against the door with arms folded. "You seemed preoccupied when I walked up. Is something on your mind?"

She can't very well tell him she was contemplating her divorce. But she would appreciate his opinion on her opening a floral design shop. "I'm contemplating a new business venture, but I have no clue what I'm doing."

"I'm intrigued. I can offer an ear if you need a sounding board."

"I'm sure you have more important things to do," she says, reaching for another bucket.

"I can spare time for a budding entrepreneur. I'll fetch us some coffee and meet you in the cafe in a few minutes."

She looks up from her task. "Coffee sounds wonderful. I prefer mine black."

"Black it is." Bruce sets a bucket in front of the door. "That should hold it open," he says and disappears around the side of the building.

Ten minutes later, when all the buckets are neatly stored away, she joins Bruce in the cafe. Servers are preparing for tastings behind the wine bars and the tables around them are set for lunch for the hordes of customers who will soon arrive.

Laney tells Bruce about her history with Sylvia and how Sylvia has grown increasingly difficult lately. "I've found a small storefront on Magnolia Avenue to lease. I'd have enough money to start the business if not for the high cost of the fixtures and refrigeration."

"Have you considered applying for a loan?"

"I've written my business proposal, and I have excellent credit.

Because of the amount, I'm worried the bank will ask for collateral. The only thing I own of value is my house, which is jointly titled with Hugh."

Bruce shrugs. "So get Hugh to co-sign on the loan."

"I'd rather not involve him. I prefer to do this on my own," Laney says, and is relieved when Bruce doesn't press her with questions about her husband.

"Okay, then. Let's see." Bruce crosses his legs and strokes his clean-shaven chin. "I assume you've gotten cost estimates from more than one source."

Laney holds up three fingers. "They're all about the same. Outrageous."

"Do the fixtures and refrigeration have to be new? Maybe you could find used equipment."

Laney's gray-blue eyes grow wide. "That's a brilliant idea, Bruce. I'll investigate it right away."

"I understand your desire to tackle this project on your own, but have you even told Hugh about this venture?" Bruce asks, his intense gaze making her squirm.

Laney shakes her head as she stares down at her coffee. "Not yet. He's not exactly the supportive type. He's worried my career will interfere with my responsibilities as a wife and mother. My goal is to build something that belongs only to me, that I don't have to share with Hugh or the girls."

Bruce gives her a nod of approval. "I admire your independence."

With a sad smile, Laney says, "That's part of the problem. I'm not at all independent. But I'm taking baby steps to branch out."

"You've gotta start somewhere. How old are your children?"

"I have two girls, Ella and Grace. They are twelve and thirteen." She shows him her phone's screensaver, a recent picture of the girls in their field hockey uniforms.

Bruce takes the phone from her and studies the picture. "They're beautiful like their mother. And on their way to being self-sufficient. They'll be going off to college soon. The flower business will occupy your time when your nest is empty."

Laney's life is lonely now. She can't imagine what it will be like when Ella and Grace leave. "Exactly. Things will be crazy for a couple of years, but once the girls start driving, I'll have even more time on my hands."

He hands her back the phone. "Talk to Hugh. He might surprise you. Doesn't every man want his wife to lead a fulfilling life?"

Every man except Hugh, Laney thinks.

She pushes back from the table. "I should get going. I have much to do to prepare for this wedding." They stand together and exit the cafe. "Thanks for the coffee. And for the advice."

Bruce's fingers graze her forearm. "You bet. Any time."

Laney feels an emptiness inside when they part. She enjoys his company. He's easygoing and supportive and sensible. All the things Hugh is not.

She spends the rest of the day in a daze, weighing the pros and cons of confiding in her husband about her floral business. After much deliberation, she decides the process will be easier and their lives will run smoother if he blesses her venture.

She rehearses her speech as she's driving the girls to their respective sleepovers. But when Hugh comes home from work in a foul mood, she puts off telling him until later.

After dinner, Laney retreats to the guest room with her laptop and stays up late searching the internet for used equipment. She hits the jackpot when she discovers a post on an online market-place from Kelly Cobb, a recently retired floral designer in Charlotte.

Laney quickly types out an email requesting more information about her offerings. Kelly's response is waiting in her inbox when she wakes a five thirty the following morning.

Laney sits straight up in bed as she reads the message. Kelly's floral design business failed due to a flooded market in Charlotte. She needs to unload a large worktable, several display fixtures, and two small refrigeration units. Kelly includes the age and dimensions of the units along with her asking price.

Laney responds. *Thank you for this information. I need a few days to work things out. I'll be back in touch soon.*

Laney showers, dresses, and stops by the kitchen for coffee to-go before hitting the road to Hope Springs. Reed Wholesale Florist is bustling despite the early hour. A sales associate, the name tag on her black apron identifying her as Cindy, leads Laney to the back corner of a refrigerated room where her prepared order awaits.

Cindy gestures at the buckets of pale pink lilies. "We couldn't get orange. You'll have to make do with pink."

"Are you kidding me? The bride's entire color scheme is based around citrus-colored flowers, which means orange and yellow lilies. Pink will not work."

Cindy lifts a shoulder. "Sorry, hon. That's the best we can do. You're not obligated to purchase them."

Panic grips Laney's chest. This can't be happening. Not today. Not for the Coleman wedding.

A petite young woman with a mop of blonde corkscrews wanders over. She looks down at the lilies and up at Cindy. "Why didn't you call your customer in advance to let her know you couldn't fill her order?"

Cindy's face beams red. "I . . . um . . ."

"That's crappy customer service, if you ask me." The curly-headed woman turns to Laney. "Don't worry. I can sell you all the orange lilies you need."

"Are you a wholesale florist?"

"Better. I'm a flower grower." The woman hands Laney a business card. "I'm Claire Davis, and my farm, Flower Fanatics, is just outside of town. I'm going there now. Tell me how many stems you need. You can stop by when you leave here, and I'll have them ready for you."

Relief floods Laney. "You're a godsend. You just saved this bride's wedding day."

Laney charges the flowers, minus the pink lilies, to Sylvia's account and loads them into the back of her Suburban. She punches the directions into her phone, and Siri guides her to the opposite side of town. She turns off the main highway and drives down a dirt road until she comes to a charming farmhouse. Under a covered area on the side are bins of flowers of every variety. Beyond the house, blooming fields stretch as far as the eye can see.

As promised, Claire has the lilies ready, packed in several large cardboard boxes for safe transport. "These are gorgeous, the prettiest I've ever seen. And you grew them yourself."

Claire nods, her corkscrew curls bouncing around on her head. "In our greenhouse. It's at a different location, further outside of town."

Laney fishes her credit card out of her wallet and hands it to Claire. "I'm from Lovely. I work with Sylvia Campbell, who usually purchases the orders for our weddings. Has she done business with you before?"

"The name doesn't ring a bell," Clair says, as she processes the charge. "Two years ago, my partner, Katherine, and I started this business for the sole purpose of supplying flowers for events at Hope Springs Farm. As we've grown, we've taken on a few select clients. Our goal is to make use of the flowers we don't need. We have no interest in becoming a wholesale florist."

"I'm considering starting a floral design business in Lovely. Would you consider taking me on as a client?"

"We would certainly consider your application," Claire says. "We like to vet our customers. I noticed your name on your credit card. Are you any relationship to the Love family at Love-Struck vineyards?"

"Yes! My husband, Hugh, is one of the owners."

"Cool. We usually start out on a trial basis. It's nothing personal. We want to make certain we don't grow beyond our means."

"I totally understand," Laney says. "I would be grateful for the opportunity to work with you. Reed Wholesale does not impress me. Their flowers are subpar, and what happened today with the lilies could've been a disaster for my bride."

As they transport the boxes of lilies to Laney's Suburban, Claire explains, "They have their product flown in from all over the world. By the time the flowers arrive, they're usually past their prime. We grow most mainstream varieties. When we need something exotic, we order straight from the grower."

"Good to know." They store the boxes in the back and Laney closes the rear door. "I don't have my business cards yet."

"No worries. I'll remember you. Come back when you're ready to do business."

"Will do. Thank you so much," Laney says with a wave as she climbs behind the wheel.

Laney wrestles with guilt on the way back to Lovely. She is plotting to steal business away from Sylvia. But that guilt turns to anger when three o'clock rolls around and Sylvia has yet to return from Charlottesville.

Laney is fastening a bouquet onto a white chiffon-draped arbor when the step ladder tips over. Bruce's strong hands grab onto her, preventing her from falling off as he straightens the ladder.

"Are you okay?" he asks, holding her arm as she climbs down off the ladder.

"Thanks to you, I am," Laney says, on the verge of a meltdown.

Bruce furrows his brow. "You seem flustered. Did something happen?"

She swipes at her eyes. "Sylvia was supposed to be here at noon. I'm way behind. I haven't even started on the bridesmaids' bouquets. It'll be a miracle if I finish in time." Laney climbs back onto the stepladder, and with Bruce's help, she fastens the bouquet onto the arbor.

"What time is the wedding?" Bruce asks.

"At six. But the photographer will start taking pictures at five."

"I know nothing about flowers, but I can offer a set of hands," he says, raising his big paws.

Laney gives him a skeptical look. "I'm desperate enough to accept your offer. You can help with the groomsmen's boutonnieres. I'll show you how to make them. They're easy," she says, and they walk together back to her makeshift workshop in the barrel building's storage room.

Laney shows him how to wire and tape the boutonnieres before starting on the bridesmaids' bouquets. While they work, they slip into easy conversation. He talks about his job of rebranding the Love-Struck's varietals, and she tells him about finding the used equipment at the florist in Charlotte.

"Thanks to your suggestion, I can start my business with no loan. Things will be tight, but I can make it work if I'm careful."

The conversation soon turns personal. Bruce speaks of his painful divorce several years ago, and Laney describes her life with two adolescent daughters. When she notices him watching her, she says, "What?"

"Your face radiates when you talk about your daughters. But then your expression darkens like a storm cloud when you speak of Hugh. I can see you're not happy in your marriage. Because I've experienced Hugh's mean streak, I feel justified in asking if you're in trouble. Is Hugh hurting you, Laney?"

Laney looks away, unable to meet his gaze. "You may know Hugh, but I don't know *you* well enough to discuss my marriage."

"Fair enough. But sometimes it's easier to talk to a stranger, and I'm here for you if you need anything at all." He pulls out his phone. "I want you to have my number. Give me yours and I'll text you mine."

Laney recites her number as his thumbs fly across the screen. He's pocketing his phone when the door swings open and Sylvia sashays in.

"Yoo-hoo! I've arrived."

Laney glances at her watch. "Four hours late. You were supposed to be here at noon."

"My daughter's flight was delayed."

Laney gestures at her phone on the worktable. "I've called you a dozen times. Why didn't you answer? You could've at least texted to let me know you would be late. I've been busting my butt here. This is the largest wedding we've ever done, Sylvia."

"And it shows. I walked through the tent on my way over. The table arrangements are gorgeous." She opens the large wine cooler where Laney has stored the completed bouquets and boutonnieres. "Looks like you've taken care of everything."

"With my friend's help." Laney's gaze travels to Bruce and back to Sylvia. "I'm tired of you taking advantage of me, Sylvia. I think it's time for us to part ways."

Sylvia's body goes rigid. "What do you mean by part ways?"

"I mean, I quit." Laney slips her apron over her head, tosses it on the table, and heads toward the door.

Sylvia hurries after her. "Wait! You can't leave now! We have to hand out the bouquets and boutonnieres. And what about the takedown after the wedding?"

"I'm sure you can manage," Laney says, motioning for Bruce to follow as she exits the storage room.

They barely make it outside before bursting into laughter. Bruce offers her a high five. "Looks like you're on your way to starting your own business."

Laney slaps his hand. "No turning back now." She gets in her car, starts the engine, and rolls down her window. "Thanks again for helping me today. I would never have made it without you."

"Anytime. I'm not a stranger, Laney. Think of me as your friend."

CHAPTER 8
DANIEL

Daniel is admiring his tuxedo-clad reflection in the mirror when he receives a text from Caroline Horton, an old high school girlfriend. *I'm in town for the Coleman wedding. Will you be there?*

He waits a few minutes before responding. *Indeed. I look forward to catching up.*

Daniel's plans for the evening are looking up. He's been lonely this week without Ruthie. Caroline was smoking hot in high school. A new romance is just what he needs to brighten up his life.

He goes to his study for a shot of whiskey before heading out. He cuts across his backyard to the winery where Casey and Sonia, his new event planner, are putting the finishing touches on the food tables under the massive sailcloth tent.

"This isn't a wedding. It's a circus. From now on, we will cap our attendance at six hundred. Are we clear on this?" Daniel says, his eyes on Sonia.

"Yes, sir! You won't get an argument from me. I would never have survived this week without Casey. I need a permanent assistant."

Her disgruntled attitude doesn't sit well with Daniel. "Ada never had any help when she was in the position."

"Then Ada is super woman, because this is too much work for one person."

"You young people don't know the meaning of hard work. That's what's wrong with your generation." Daniel turns to Casey. "Hire an assistant. Get someone older with more experience. We'll make that person the lead and Sonia the assistant."

"No, we won't either," Casey says in a warning tone. "Sonia is perfectly capable of being the lead. She's doing an excellent job. We're all just a little on edge."

Daniel softens. "You're right. We bit off more than we can chew with this wedding." He holds Casey at arm's length. "You look stunning, by the way. The dress suits you," he says of her lavender ruffled frock.

Casey flashes him her kilowatt smile. "You look rather dashing yourself."

"Is Luke coming tonight?" Daniel asks, brushing a stray strand of hair off her cheek.

"He's already here somewhere."

When Casey returns her attention to the tables, Daniel stands watching the wedding guests arrive in their finery. The sight of Ada in a burnt orange dress that clings to her slim figure takes his breath away. Daniel moves closer but waits until Enzo goes to the bar for drinks before approaching Ada. "You look amazing. That color really suits you."

Ada flinches when he kisses her cheek, and she says in a curt tone, "Hello, Daniel."

He sweeps an arm at the party. "This is quite the spectacle, isn't it? John and Alice Coleman have spared no expense for their only daughter. You and Enzo will soon get married. We've always talked about having your wedding here. I would love to give you that wedding if you're interested. You can have anything you want. The sky's the limit. I will be one proud father walking you down the aisle."

The gold flecks in Ada's brown eyes flash with anger. "You disowned me a month ago, and now you want to play father of the bride? I'm sorry, Daniel. But I can't just forget the way you treated me. Excuse me," she says and strides angrily off through the crowd.

Daniel watches her go before making his way to the area of the lawn where the ceremony will take place. He finds a seat on the aisle, and twenty minutes later, he watches John Coleman hand his beautiful daughter over to her handsome groom at the altar.

Daniel reminds himself that it's not the end of the world. He still has Casey's wedding to plan for. It won't be long before his golden-haired love child marries her saxophone player. As quickly as his spirits soar, they sink again. He loves Casey, but she can't take Ada's place in his heart.

After the ceremony, Daniel makes a beeline back to the bar for a drink. He's waiting in line when his longtime friend and concierge doctor, Jason Harmon, pulls him out of earshot of the other guests.

Jason speaks to him in a loud whisper. "My office has been trying to reach you. Time is of the essence, Daniel. Since you've been avoiding me, I had my staff schedule your procedure with a top-notch surgical oncologist for this coming Wednesday. You'll have the operation at UVA's University Hospital. Plan to stay at least two nights. You'll need someone with you. Have you spoken with your family about your condition?"

"They don't need to know about this. And you'd better not tell them either."

Jason shrugs. "That's your choice. I'll go along with it for now. As long as you stop pretending you don't have cancer and face this thing head on."

Daniel considers the bumpy road ahead—surgery, recovery, and follow-up treatment. Weeks have passed since his diagnosis. He was hoping it would all go away. "I'm not ready, Jason. I need a little more time."

"Time is the one thing you don't have. I had to pull strings to get you in with Dr. Olson. I assume you want the best."

Daniel lets out a deep sigh. "What I want is to not have cancer."

"That's what we're hoping for. The sooner we go after it, the better." Jason slaps him on the back. "Let's get this ball rolling. Call my office first thing Monday morning and schedule your pre-op exam for Monday afternoon or Tuesday."

As Daniel watches Jason disappear into the crowd, he wonders for the umpteenth time if he should tell his family about the cancer. Then again, what's the point in making them worry unnecessarily? He'll wait until after the surgery before deciding how to proceed.

He's scanning the crowd when his eyes meet those of an attractive brunette in a black evening gown, a dress more appropriate for the opera than a wedding. The years have been good to Caroline Horton. She's trim with toned muscles. If she ever had facial wrinkles, a plastic surgeon has expertly removed them.

"Caroline." He extends his arms, and when she walks into them, his memory takes him back to his freshman year of high school. Once they lost their virginities to each other, they had sex every chance they got—in the back seats of cars, in the woods around Love-Struck, in her bedroom late at night while her parents slept.

"You look lovely," he says when he pulls away. "How long has it been since you were last in town?"

"Decades. And I haven't missed it a bit. But the bride is my godchild. I had to come for her sake."

Daniel had forgotten Caroline was best childhood friends with the bride's mother. "I'm sure Alice appreciates you being here."

"I don't think she even noticed I'm here." Caroline palms the side of his face. "Truth be told, I came to see you, Daniel. A girl never forgets her first love. I've thought about you a lot over the years. How long has it been since Lila died?"

"Thirteen years. I remember reading about Sam on social media. When did he die?"

Caroline's smile fades, and she lowers her hand from his face. "Six years ago."

Daniel grabs two champagne flutes from a passing server. "Tonight is a joyous occasion. Let's celebrate." He touches his glass to hers. "To old times."

"To old times," she says, a naughty smile creeping onto her lips as she sips.

Daniel gulps down his champagne. It's been a long time since he flirted with a woman, and he's out of practice. "So, what're you up to these days? Are you still in New York?"

"Of course! I'm committed to too many nonprofit organizations to ever leave. Not that I would ever want to. I've got my finger on the pulse of the city."

Daniel had forgotten how melodramatic Caroline could be. "Good for you."

As Caroline rambles on about her important friends and volunteer work, Daniel grows bored, and his eyes roam the crowd. He does a double take when he spots Ruthie, looking so elegant he almost didn't recognize her. Her emerald dress drapes her curves, and a slit up the leg shows off her shapely thigh. Instead of the usual rat's nest perched on top of her head, her blonde hair is smoothed back in an understated knot.

Daniel burns with anger when Bud appears at Ruthie's side and places a possessive hand on the small of her back. The rotten bastard. First, he stole Daniel's daughter and now his mistress.

He touches Caroline's arm. "Excuse me a minute. I need to attend to some business. Help yourself to the food. I'll be back soon."

Daniel makes his way through the wedding guests to the lawn, skirts the tent, and reenters the crowd closer to where Ruthie and Bud are standing with Enzo and Ada. He spies on them from a distance, pretending to graze the buffet while picking up on snippets of their conversation. Best he can tell, they are talking about horses. How boring. Why would Ruthie go out with him?

Ada drags Enzo onto the dance floor, and Bud ventures off to the bar for drink refills, leaving Ruthie standing by herself. Daniel sneaks up behind her and whispers in her ear. "What're you doing here?"

If Ruthie is surprised to see him, she doesn't show it. "I'm here as Bud Malone's plus-one. Not that it's any of your business."

"Why the sudden interest in Bud? Are you trying to get back at me by going out with Ada's baby daddy?"

"Don't be vulgar, Daniel. For your information, Bud's been asking me out for years. I've always turned him down because I was in hiding with you. But I'm enjoying myself. He's a proper gentleman. And he's attentive. He's not embarrassed to be seen with me."

Her insults sting, but he refrains from responding. The creamy skin on her neck entices him, and he leans in close, inhaling her familiar rose-scented body lotion. "I've missed you this week, Ruthie. Can we go somewhere and talk?"

Ruthie cranes her neck to look back at him. "Go where? To some dark corner of the party where no one will see the great Daniel Love conversing with common white trash."

"Don't be like this, Ruthie?"

She spins on her stiletto heels to face him. "You're annoying me, Daniel. Please leave before I scream and cause a scene."

His hands fly up as he backs away. "Suit yourself."

Daniel fights his way to the bar and downs two shots of scotch before going in search of Caroline. He finds her chatting the ear off one of her old schoolmates.

He pulls her aside. "There are too many people here. Let's go next door to my house. We can have drinks by the pool."

She walks her fingers up his chest. "I thought you'd never ask. We can go skinny-dipping in the moonlight."

Bright sunlight streams through the french doors in Daniel's bedroom, casting Caroline in an unflattering glow. She's not nearly as pretty in the light of day. And her breath smells like a gorilla's armpits. His face warms remembering the things they'd done in his pool and later his bed. He'd forgotten about her unsavory reputation in high school, how she'd slept around with many of his friends after they'd broken up. Her disreputable habits appeared to have followed her into adulthood. Thank goodness he thought to use condoms.

He gently nudges her. "Caroline, you need to get up. I have a tee time in an hour. I can drop you at your hotel on the way to the club."

She draws the covers under her chin. "I didn't book a hotel."

His eyes narrow. "Where were you planning to sleep?"

She runs her big toe down his leg. "With you, of course."

And Daniel fell right into her trap. "Did you bring any clothes with you? Or did you wear your evening gown on the airplane?"

"Don't be ridiculous. I have a bag in my rental car. I parked at the winery. My flight isn't until later this afternoon. Run along to your golf game, and I'll hang out here until time to go to the airport."

"Like hell you will." He flings the covers back, exposing her naked body. Her belly is white and flabby, not tanned and tone like Ruthie's. "Give me your keys. I'll get your car for you, and you can shower here, but then you need to leave."

She props herself on both elbows. "Why are you being such a grump?"

He holds his hand out. "Give me the keys."

"Fine. I'll get them for you." She takes the covers with her when she rolls out of bed. She retrieves her purse from across the room and tosses him the keys.

Eager to get away from this woman, Daniel disappears into his walk-in closet, changes into sweats, and hurries from the room.

Icy dread overcomes him as he walks next door to the winery. He really screwed up with Ruthie. She looked so beautiful last night. Maybe he was mistaken about her. Maybe she could fit into his world after all. Why does her background even matter when she makes him happy? He'll get on his knees and beg for Ruthie's forgiveness. After he gets through the cancer surgery.

CHAPTER 9
ADA

"We should think about hiring an interior designer," Ada suggests to Enzo on the way to visit a dairy farm on Sunday afternoon.

Enzo glances over at her from behind the wheel of his pickup. "Why do we need a decorator when the house is perfect as is?"

"Most of the rooms could use a fresh coat of paint. A decorator can help us pick out paint colors and give us guidance on combining our furnishings."

He lifts his hands off the steering wheel, letting her know he won't argue. "Whatever you want is fine by me. I'm staying out of it."

"How'd did I get so lucky?" Ada stretches across the console to kiss his cheek. "I love you, Enzo Medici."

He smiles at her. "And I love you."

Ada settles back in her seat. "I still can't believe we got the house," she says, and for the rest of the hour-long drive, they discuss the logistics of taking ownership of their new home.

Shady Creek Creamery is a small farm located just outside of Roanoke. The owner, Sally West, a middle-aged woman with a large frame and shock of bright red hair, is waiting for them on the front stoop of her quaint farmhouse.

"I set up the tasting in the barn." She gestures at the red rustic barn at the end of the short gravel drive. "Head on back, and I'll meet you there."

The tasting comprises artisan goat cheeses produces by Shady Creek Creamery. Sally offers them samples of normal cheeses like feta and blue and chèvre and a host of varieties Ada has never heard about.

"I'm impressed," Ada says. "I consider myself a cheese snob, and you have way exceeded my expectations."

Sally beams. "I'll give you a considerable discount and provide free once-a-week delivery if we can work out an exclusive agreement."

Ada taps her chin as she considers her proposal. "I can promise not to sell other goat cheeses. However, for the sake of variety, I'll plan to offer some cow cheeses."

"Of course," Sally says. "And I know a few farmers who make the top-quality artisan cow cheese. I'm happy to provide their names."

Ada looks over at Enzo, who shrugs, leaving the decision to Ada. "Can you agree not to sell your cheeses through any retailer within a fifty-mile radius of my wine shop?"

"Hmm. I don't know about that. You're asking a lot."

"After six months, if you're not satisfied with our sales, we'll reassess the situation."

Sally hesitates a minute before extending her hand. "That sounds fair. We have a deal."

Ada walks toward the barn door. "We're hoping to open on October first. I can confirm that date in the next week." She loops her arm through Enzo's. "We'd love for you to be at the celebration."

"That's exciting. I'll come if I can."

Sally walks them to the truck, and they wave to her as they drive off.

Ada offers Enzo a high five. "This is so exciting! We got our own exclusive farmstead cheese line."

He grins as he makes a left-hand turn onto the highway. "Who knew you were such a tough negotiator?"

"I learned a thing or two from Daniel over the years."

A mile down the road, Ada's phone vibrates with a call from Bud. "Ada, you need to get over to the equestrian center now. There's something wrong with Glory."

The bottom falls out of Ada's stomach. "What do you mean? What's wrong with her?"

"She's exhibiting signs of colic. I've already called the vet. She's on the way."

Ada glances over at her fiancé. "Enzo and I are leaving a cheese tasting in Roanoke. We're an hour away. We'll be there as soon as we can."

"I'll call you if anything changes," Bud says.

Ada drops the phone in her lap. "Drive faster. Glory's sick."

Enzo looks at Ada with concern in his dark eyes. "Sick, how?"

"Bud thinks it's colic," Ada says and turns away from him.

Leaning her head against the window, she closes her eyes and prays for Glory's recovery. Sixty minutes feels like sixty hours, but they finally arrive back in Lovely around five thirty. They pass the vet's pickup truck as they are pulling into the equestrian center.

Enzo parks his truck, and they hurry into the stable to find Bud standing outside Glory's stall, cooing encouraging words to her.

The sight of her horse lying on her side with labored breathing tugs at Ada's heartstrings. "What did the vet say?"

"Lindsay's not convinced it's colic. She drew some blood. We should have the results in a couple of hours." Bud turns away from the stall. "It's gonna be a long night. I'll make us some coffee."

Ada presses her face against the stall bars. "Go home, Enzo. There's nothing you can do here."

Enzo places a reassuring hand on her shoulder. "I'm not leaving you, Ada."

The minutes tick off the clock. If she's this concerned about her horse, what will it be like when their child is ill? At least, she'll have Enzo by her side. And Enzo makes everything better.

Bud returns from the house with a thermos of coffee and a small basket of warm ham biscuits. Ada is too worried to eat, but Enzo gobbles down three.

It's almost eight o'clock when the vet returns. "We detected arsenic in Glory's blood," Lindsay says with a troubled expression. "We'll need to test your water supply, but since none of the other horses are sick, we have to consider the possibility someone poisoned her."

Ada gasps, and Bud tenses. "Who would do such a thing?"

Hot flashes of anger surge through Ada's body. "Stuart did this."

Bud turns toward Ada, his face set in stone. "That's a very serious allegation, Ada. Why would you say such a thing?"

Three sets of eyes are on her, waiting for her answer. "Because he threatened me."

"Excuse us a minute." Bud takes Ada by the arm and marches her out the back of the stable. "When and how did Stuart threaten you?"

"On Thursday. He was waiting for me in the parking lot after you and I met."

"And what did he say?"

Ada thinks back to the encounter. "I don't remember his exact words. But he's upset you're leaving me the equestrian center. He thinks it's rightfully his."

"How does he know about that? Did you tell him?"

Ada shakes her head. "Enzo is the only person I told. Stuart threatened to make my life miserable if I don't disclaim the property."

Bud pulls a hand down his face. "I'm sorry, Ada, but I find this hard to believe. Stuart is not a vengeful man."

"Naturally, you would believe your legitimate child over me."

"I'm not taking anyone's side, Ada. But I think maybe you misinterpreted what he said. I know my son."

Ada grits her teeth. "And I know what I heard. By the way, I don't want your farm. And I don't want to work for you either." She brushes past him on her way back inside.

"How are we going to treat her?" Ada asks Lindsay who is in the stall, kneeling beside Glory.

"We aren't." Lindsay gets to her feet and emerges from the stall. "The poison will eventually work itself out of her system. In the meantime, I've given her medicine to help ease the symptoms."

Bud joins them. "Should someone stay with her tonight to monitor her?"

Lindsay stuffs her stethoscope into her backpack. "She should be fine. She just needs to rest. Call me if she isn't feeling better by morning."

"Don't worry, I will," Ada says. "Thank you so much for coming to our rescue on a Sunday night."

Lindsay offers her a warm smile. "You bet. Get some sleep. There's nothing you can do for her here."

Ada spends a few minutes with Glory while Enzo and Bud speak in hushed tones outside the stall.

"What did Bud say to you?" Ada asks on the drive home.

"He's worried about you, and he's going to talk to Stuart."

"He's wasting his time. Stuart will only deny it," Ada says as tears blur her vision.

Enzo takes her hand. "Why didn't you tell me Stuart threatened you?"

Ada wipes a tear off her cheek. "Because I'm tired of family drama. I've had enough from the Loves to last a lifetime. I'm sure you're sick of hearing about it anyway."

Enzo brings her hand to his lips. "Not at all. You can always come to me with your problems. That's what being in a relationship is all about."

"I don't know what I'd do without you." She moves closer to him and rests her head on his shoulder. "Bud is right about one thing. I've known Stuart since we were kids, and he never seemed like the vengeful type. I made the mistake of not taking him seriously. And now Glory is paying for my mistake."

"Maybe Stuart isn't the one who poisoned Glory."

Ada's phone lights up with a text from Stuart. "Here's the proof we need," Ada says, and reads the text aloud to Enzo. "Boo hoo. I heard Glory is under the weather. Next time, she won't be so lucky."

"You need to show that to Bud," Enzo says, jabbing a finger at her phone.

Ada lets out a heavy sigh. "I'm not a tattletale, Enzo. I should never have said anything to Bud in the first place. The last thing I want to do is come between Stuart and Bud. I thought things would be different this time around. Why can't I have a normal family with loving parents and siblings?"

"Every family has its issues, Ada. Even mine, and I was an only child. Your troubled past will make you a better parent when the time comes."

"Damn straight! We'll teach our children that family comes first and to always look out for one another."

Enzo smiles over at her. "There's that fighting spirit I love."

CHAPTER 10
LANEY

Laney is ready to move forward with her business venture. She's negotiated an affordable price on used equipment, established a source for wholesale flowers, and devised a stringent but workable budget. All she needs is Hugh's approval before she signs the lease. She doesn't want his money, but she could use his support. She'll be working long hours at first, until she can afford an assistant. There will be times, primarily on the weekends, when he'll have to pick up the slack at home.

On Monday evening, for the first time in years, she prepares his favorite dinner of lamb chops and homemade garlic mashed potatoes.

"What's all this?" he asks, when he sees the table set with their fine china and a bouquet of roses. "Are you going to pester me about marriage counseling again?"

"Not marriage counseling." She sits down opposite him at the kitchen table. "But I have something else I need to discuss with you."

Hugh rolls his eyes. "Great. Where are the girls?"

"They have a team dinner to rally enthusiasm for their big game against Hope Springs High School tomorrow. They'll be home in a while."

He unfolds his linen napkin and places it in his lap. "So, what do you need to talk to me about?"

"Let's pray first," she says, and offers their family's simple blessing.

"Out with it," Hugh says, brandishing his knife at her. "If you're buttering me up to redecorate the living room, you have my permission."

She drags her fork through her potatoes. "I redecorated the living room last year. In fact, I've recently refurbished every room in this house."

Recognition crosses his face. "I get it. You want to move into a bigger house."

"Hugh, please! Be quiet and let me explain." She inhales a deep breath. "I'm starting a floral design business. I've done a lot of soul searching these past few weeks. My unhappiness isn't just about our marital problems. I've dedicated the past twenty years to meeting your needs and the needs of our daughters. I want more out of life than being a stay-at-home mom." Her hand shoots up before he can argue. "Don't misunderstand me. I was blessed to have had these years with the girls, but Ella and Grace will go off to college soon. What will I do with my time, then?"

Hugh grunts as he shovels potatoes in his mouth. "That's years from now. We'll worry about it when it happens."

Laney pushes her plate away and reaches for her wineglass. "I'm worried about it now. I want to build a career for myself, to work and earn my own money. I'm tired of cooking and cleaning."

"Then hire a housekeeper."

"I plan to." She runs a thumb around the rim of her wineglass. "I need to challenge myself. Use the creative skills God gave me."

"If you're asking for money, you've come to the wrong place. It's too risky. You know nothing about running a business."

"But I know plenty about flowers." She cocks her head. "I don't want your money. But maybe you can give me some advice about the business side of things."

He levels his gaze on her. "Is that what you want from me? To do your accounting?"

"I want nothing from you, Hugh, except your support. God willing, I'll be crazy busy at the shop. You'll need to help with carpooling. I may ask you to pick up takeout and go to the girl's games if I can't make it. You should do that anyway. You haven't been to a one since school started."

"I have an important career, Laney."

"Ha. You work for yourself. You can leave anytime you want."

He stares down at his plate. "Where do you plan to operate this business? I won't have strange people coming in and out of my house."

Laney stares at him as if he's lost his mind. "Give me some credit, Hugh. I'm not opening a floral shop in our home. There's a small storefront for lease in the building next to Ruthie's Diner."

"And what will you use for working capital?" he asks, stuffing a bite of lamb into his mouth.

"The money I've saved from doing wedding flowers."

"I see. And how much money is that?" She answers him truthfully, and for the next few minutes, he barrages her with questions, attempting to shoot holes in her business plan. But she has her answers ready.

He sets down his utensils and picks up his whiskey tumbler. For a long minute, he studies her with an expression she can't read. He drains the brown liquid and sets down the tumbler. "I'm sorry, Laney. I can't give you my permission. You lack the drive to run your own business."

Laney stands abruptly, knocking the chair over. "You know nothing about me and what I'm capable of. You stopped caring about me the day we got married." She snatches up their dinner plates. "I wasn't asking for your permission anyway. And I don't need your blessing."

He stands to face her. "Like hell you don't. When your venture fails, I'll be the one to bail you out."

"I have no intention of failing. I'm doing this thing, and you can't stop me." Laney drops the plates in the sink and runs down the hall. She's halfway up the stairs when Hugh grabs her ankle and pulls her back down.

He jerks her to her feet. "If I wanted a businesswoman for a wife, I would've married one. If you move forward with this, I'll divorce you."

A smirk appears on her lips. "Promise?"

He balls up his fist and draws his hand back as though he's going to punch her.

"Do it!" she says, bracing herself. "And I'll go straight to the police."

He lowers his fist, and she backs away. "So, you'll give me a divorce?"

He bares his teeth at her and snarls, "Not on your life."

"You no longer control my life." Laney races up the stairs to the guest room. She falls back on the bed and stares up at the ceiling while her heart rate steadies. Hugh has threatened to hit her before, but he always stops himself. He's aware of Virginia's strict grounds for divorce, physical abuse being one of them.

Laney curls herself into a ball and has a good cry. What did she ever see in Hugh in the first place? And how will she get herself out of this mess of a marriage?

When she hears the girls come in, she wishes them goodnight before putting on her pajamas and getting ready for bed. She tosses and turns, but she can't fall asleep. She needs to talk. She remembers that Bruce had given her his number, and the parting words he said. *I'm not a stranger, Laney. Think of me as your friend.*

When he answers on the third ring, she says, "Hey, Bruce. It's Laney. I'm sorry to be calling so late."

"Are you okay, Laney? You sound like you've been crying."

She tells him about her argument with Hugh. "I feel like my soul is drowning. I can't take this life anymore. What am I supposed to do, Bruce?"

"You save your soul. Starting your own business is the first step in doing that."

"Hugh's convinced I'll fail. What do you think?"

"As long as you believe in yourself, and I'm absolutely certain you do, your business will thrive."

"Thanks for your vote of confidence." Laney rolls over onto her side. "Why do I care so much about what he thinks? Why do I feel I need his approval?"

"Because he's conditioned you to feel that way. But with my help and a lot of positive self-talk, we're going to recondition you. First thing in the morning, you call the building's owner and sign the lease."

She giggles. "Yes, sir."

They talk for a few minutes longer. When they finally hang up, Laney is too excited to sleep. Staring up at the ceiling, she gives herself a pep talk, convincing herself she can do anything she sets her mind to.

She wakes before her alarm sounds, feeling stronger and more self-assured than she has in years. When she hears Hugh leave, she throws on exercise clothes, makes pancakes for the girls, and sees them to the bus stop. But instead of going for her walk, she returns home to call Diana Gladstone.

"Diana, this is Laney Love. I'm finally ready to sign the lease." An awkward silence fills the line. "Hello? Diana, are you there? Is the storefront still available?"

"As of this morning, I have an offer on the building. I hate to be the one to spoil the surprise, but the prospective buyer is your husband. I assume he's giving the building to you as a gift, so you can open your flower shop."

"Actually, Diana, he's buying the building to prevent me from opening the flower shop."

Diana lets out an audible gasp. "Are you sure about that? He seemed so excited."

"I'm positive. I discussed it with him last night. He's adamantly opposed to me starting a business."

"Why that rotten bastard. I don't have to sell the building. The storefront is yours. I'll have the lease drawn up right away."

Laney's spirits soar. "Do you really mean it?"

Diana chuckles. "I really mean it. I will take great pleasure in turning down your husband's offer."

CHAPTER 11
DANIEL

Daniel asks Marabella to join him for a cup of coffee at breakfast on Tuesday morning.

She plants a hand on her hip. "Am I in trouble, Mr. Love?"

Daniel chuckles. "You? In trouble? Of course not. I have a delicate situation I need your help with."

"In that case, let me get my coffee." She pours herself a mug and sits down at the table with him. "What's the matter, Mr. Love?"

"I'm having a medical procedure on Wednesday to remove malignant polyps on my colon."

Marabella scrunches up her face. "By malignant, do you mean cancer?"

"Unfortunately. If the surgery goes well, I won't need follow-up treatment. I've decided not to tell my family until I understand more about my prognosis. There's no reason to upset them unnecessarily. Can I count on your discretion?"

"Absolutely, Mr. Love. Mum's the word," Marabella says, dragging an imaginary zipper across her lips.

"I'm having the surgery at UVA in Charlottesville. I'll need someone with me while I'm in the hospital and for a few days when I come home. I've called every local at-home nursing service in town. None of them have any certified nursing assistants available. Do you, by any chance, know of someone?"

Marabella bobs her gray cropped head. "I do. My nephew, Claude, is a CNA. And he is available. His previous employer passed away on Sunday. God rest the man's soul."

"Excellent." Daniel checks his watch. "I need to leave for a doctor's appointment. If you text me Claude's number, I'll call him on the way."

"Yes, sir," Marabella says, standing with him.

Daniel pours the rest of his coffee into a to-go cup and leaves the house. On the drive to town, he has a brief but pleasant phone conversation with Claude and hires him on the spot.

After enduring an hour of torture at the doctor's office, he stops by the diner to see Ruthie. He takes a seat at the counter, front and center, where she can't miss him. But she ignores him anyway.

He flags her down and hollers, "Hey, Ruthie! Can I get some service, please?"

Every eye in the diner is on her as she wanders over, notepad in hand. "What do you want?"

"You," he says with a grin.

She glares at him with cold blue eyes. "Seriously, Daniel. I'm busy. I don't have time for your games. Are you ordering food or just taking up space?"

"I'll have coffee, please."

She slams a mug on the counter in front of him and fills it with steaming coffee from a pot.

"How was your date with Bud? Are the two of you seeing each other now?"

"It's too early to predict where things will lead." She returns the pot to the coffeemaker. "We enjoy each other's company. He's cooking dinner for me on Wednesday. Imagine that, Daniel. He invited me to his house for dinner on the second date. Not after ten years of sleeping together."

"You didn't waste any time moving on."

"Nor did you. An attractive brunette was in here yesterday, bragging about how she lured the infamous Daniel Love into her bed on Saturday night. I believe she said her name was Caroline. An old high school girlfriend, if I remember correctly."

Daniel's face warms. "Can you blame me? I needed comforting after I saw you with Bud."

"Give me a break," Ruthie says and moves to the other end of the counter to assist another customer.

When she returns, Daniel says, "You know our history. Why'd you have to pick Bud?"

"I didn't pick him. He picked me. I told you, he's been asking me out for years. This might come as a surprise to you, Daniel, but lots of men find me attractive. Even though you don't."

"Don't be ridiculous. I think you're smoking hot, and you know it." He grabs her hand. "Give me another chance, Ruthie. I promise things will be different this time."

"Different, how? Will you take me on dates in public places?"

Daniel hesitates. "Sure, if it means that much to you."

"Can we talk about getting married?"

"You know how I feel about marriage."

She jerks her hand away. "And you know how I feel about being alone in my old age. We've reached a stalemate and gone our separate ways. No sense dragging it out."

"I'm not giving up, Ruthie," he says, sliding off his stool.

She holds out her hand. "That'll be three dollars and fifty cents."

He stares at her hand and back at her. "Put it on my tab."

"Your tab is permanently closed. I mailed your last bill this morning."

He digs a five-dollar bill out of his wallet and slaps it in her palm. "Keep the change."

She eyes the paper bill. "How generous of you."

Daniel is exiting the diner when he spots Ada outside her wine shop on the opposite corner, the white lettering on the black awning above her reading Primo Vino.

He waits for traffic to clear before darting across the street to her. "Hey, honey! I love the name you've chosen for the business. Can I peek inside?"

"Now's not a good time. As you can see, there's a lot of work in progress at the moment." Ada gestures at the store, which is crawling with workers inside and out.

Cupping his hands around his eyes, he looks in the window at the handsome black cabinetry being installed. "Very nice. Is there anything you need, anything I can do for you? I'd love to help."

"We're good. But thanks."

"Come on, Ada," he says, pulling her in for a half hug. "Are you going to stay mad at me forever?"

She pushes him away. "I don't know about forever. But definitely for the foreseeable future."

"At least there's hope." When he kisses the top of her head, she grimaces. "I'll let you get back to work."

With shoulders slumped, Daniel crosses the street to his car. He knows Ada better than she knows herself. She'll eventually forgive him. He just needs to try harder. Once he gets through the surgery, he'll wage a full-on campaign to win her back.

———

Daniel takes an immediate liking to Claude. His pearly white teeth stand out against his dark skin, and his brown eyes are big and round and warm. He's well-spoken and intelligent and he doesn't talk much.

As a team of doctors and nurses prep Daniel for his procedure, he finds Claude's quiet presence comforting. Daniel won't admit it, but he's apprehensive about both the surgery and the outcome.

Hours later, Daniel is still groggy from anesthesia when his oncologist stops by his hospital room to check on him. "Everything went well. It appears we got all the cancer, although we'll have a better idea of what we're dealing with when we receive the pathology report."

Daniel opens his mouth to speak, but his tongue is heavy, and his words mumbled.

"When can we expect the results?" Claude asks.

"Late tomorrow afternoon or Friday morning. If all goes as planned, I'll release Mr. Love from the hospital at that time," the doctor says, and excuses himself from the room.

Daniel is not an idle man. Staying in bed is worse than the pain from his surgery. He spends most of his time fretting about the results of the pathology report. If the doctor recommends chemotherapy, Daniel will have to tell his family about the cancer. How will they react? More importantly, how will Ada and Ruthie respond? Will they be sympathetic?

An idea takes hold in Daniel's mind and grows. He's almost disappointed when the doctor gives him the good news on Friday morning.

"The margins are good. It appears we got all the cancer. I see no point in doing chemo or radiation."

"Are you sure?" Daniel asks.

"Positive. You're good to go. Your release papers are in the works. We'll have you out of here within the hour."

"Thank you, Doctor," Daniel says, shaking the man's hand.

Daniel says little on the drive home to Lovely. He's relieved he doesn't need chemo or radiation. Nobody wants to go through that hell. But he's approached the situation all wrong. Instead of keeping his condition from his family, he should've been milking his diagnosis. But it's not too late. When he's feeling better in a few days, he'll call his family together and break the news.

CHAPTER 12
LANEY

Laney meets with Diana on Friday morning to sign the lease and discuss the changes she'd like to make to the storefront. She shows Diana the paint samples—a rich creamy color for the walls and a subtle yellow-green for the accents and front door.

"I love your choices," Diana says. "A fresh coat of paint will brighten things up."

"I'm glad you approve." Laney stuffs the color swatches in her bag. "A graphic designer is creating a logo for my brand, Laney's Bouquets. Are you okay with me putting a decal on the window?"

"That's perfectly fine! And I love the name you've chosen."

Laney's smile fades. "Thank you again for turning Hugh's offer down."

Diana flaps her hand, dismissing her gratitude. "No need to thank me. My first husband was a real jerk. He verbally and physically abused me. I was blessed to have supportive parents. They picked me up and set me on the right path. I hope you have someone you can lean on."

"I have a friend who's a good listener," Laney says about Bruce. "We often text or talk on the phone."

"Friends are important in troubled times. After my divorce, I found it therapeutic to help other women in abusive marriages. I've mentored many over the years. I'd be delighted to do the same with you."

"That means a lot. Thank you." Laney moves to the window so Diana can't see the tears welling in her eyes. "I know how much you want to sell the building. Maybe another buyer will come along."

"Actually, I've taken it off the market. And I'm holding off on renting it through Airbnb."

Laney spins around. "Why would you do that?"

Diana's lips part in a sympathetic smile. "I want to keep it open for you, in case you find yourself in need of a place to live. Would you like to see it?"

Laney shakes her head. "I can't afford an apartment right now, Diana. Maybe in a few months."

"The rent's not important. I want you to have a safe place to go in the event something happens."

Laney thinks back to Monday night. She can still feel Hugh's hand around her ankle, dragging her down the stairs.

Diana closes the gap between them. "I want to help you, Laney. At least let me show you the apartment."

"All right," Laney says in a reluctant tone. "I guess it won't hurt to see it."

"Good." Diana leads her out the back door and up a set of stairs to the apartment.

Laney immediately feels at home when she steps into the sunny living room. Reclaimed pine floors provide a warm backdrop for the neutral furnishings. A sofa and two chairs are slipcovered in white canvas while sheer drapes provide privacy at the four floor-to-ceiling windows. The kitchen is compact but updated with all new appliances, countertops, and cabinetry. Upstairs are two ample-sized bedrooms, each having its own tiled bathroom with a walk-in shower.

"It's lovely, Diana. And you're right. Knowing I have a place to escape offers peace of mind."

Diana presses a key in her hand. "Use it whenever you'd like. Since I'm so seldom in town, you'd be doing me a favor if you'd at least check on things now and then. One never knows when a pipe might spring a leak."

"I can do that." Laney wraps her fingers around the key. "I appreciate your generosity. But I can't ask you to hold it for me indefinitely."

Diana lifts a shoulder in an indifferent shrug. "We'll give it until the end of the year. If things have settled down for you at home, I'll list it on Airbnb in January."

"You're so kind. Thank you. Hopefully, I will have sorted out my marital problems by then."

Diana embraces her. "You're going through a rough time right now. But I promise there are better days ahead."

They lock up the apartment and return to the shop. Laney is seeing Diana off at the front door when her cell rings with a call from Love-Struck Vineyard. She waves at Diana and accepts the call.

"Thank heavens I caught you," Sonia blurts. "Are you by any chance free to do flowers for a wedding tomorrow? I realize it's last minute, but Sylvia just bailed on us."

Laney freezes, her hand on the front doorknob. "What do you mean she bailed on you?"

"She has some kind of family emergency. I can't believe she'd do this. Please say you're available. I'm freaking out right now," Sonia says, sounding hysterical.

Laney's mind races as she paces the floor. She can't afford to turn down such an opportunity if she wants to build her business. "I need more information before I commit."

"It's an average-size wedding, nothing over the top. The bride isn't picky about the flowers, only she doesn't want Gerber daisies or carnations. White flowers for the ceremony and autumn colors for the reception. Ten small table arrangements and two large ones for the buffet. Eight bridesmaids' bouquets and ten boutonnieres."

"I should be able to handle an event that size. Email me the contract with the specifics."

In the background, Laney hears Sonia typing on the keyboard. "Coming your way now. I owe you one, Laney. Let me know how I can help."

When Laney opens her laptop on the counter, the email is waiting in her inbox. She's blown away by the amount of money she stands to make on this wedding. The vineyard will take a slight percentage, and she'll have to pay for the flowers, but she'll easily bank several thousand dollars. Fury surges through Laney at the pittance Sylvia has been paying her for years.

Laney makes a few sketches before placing a call to Claire Davis at Flower Fanatics in Hope Springs. "I'm in a bit of a bind," she says, and tells Claire about her predicament.

She's relieved when Claire says, "We can easily handle an order that size. I'll have it ready for you late this afternoon."

Laney grabs her purse, locks the back door, and takes off to Hope Springs on a shopping spree. Her mind wanders during the drive, and she thinks about the apartment key zipped into the side pocket of her purse. The situation between Laney and Hugh has gone from bad to worse. They had their nastiest argument to date when she confronted him about making an offer on Diana's building. Hugh's patience is growing thin. One whiskey too many will send him over the edge. Thanks to Diana, she has somewhere to flee.

She's not sure where Bruce fits in, only that he's becoming an increasingly important person in her life. If she's not careful, her feelings for him could easily develop into something more than friendship. They have much in common, and he seems to genuinely care about her. The last thing she needs is a romantic affair to further complicate her life. While she can't stand to be in the same room with Hugh, she's still his wife, and she would never cheat on him. To make matters worse, Bruce works for Laney's father-in-law, and she can't let him risk his career.

———

Laney arrives at the vineyard early on Saturday morning and works straight through lunch. When she pushes her loaded cart over to the reception tent, a frazzled Sonia rushes over to help her with the table arrangements.

"These are amazing, Laney. Thanks for coming to our rescue. Here! Let me help." Sonia snatches up an arrangement, disheveling the flowers.

"I've got this," Laney says, taking the glass cube from her. "I'm sure you have plenty else to attend to."

"If you only knew the half of it. This job is too much for me. There are so many moving parts."

Laney offers her a smile of encouragement. "Relax, Sonia. You're doing a great job."

"I appreciate you saying that, even if it's not true." Sonia busies herself with placing pillar candles in hurricane globes. "By the way, what happened between you and Sylvia? I thought you two were a team."

"Ha. Some team. I did all the work, and she made all the money." Laney sets the arrangement down on a nearby table. "I'm not sure she can handle the business alone. If I were you, I'd confirm with her well in advance of the events you have coming up."

"You know it. After what she did today, I definitely will."

Laney tweaks the flowers to her liking. "Coincidentally, I'm starting my own floral business. If Sylvia cancels on you again, I'd be happy to take over the contract."

Sonia gives her a thumbs-up. "For sure. And we will add you to the list for future events. You're easier and way more fun to work with than Sourpuss Sylvia." She finishes with the candles and hurries off to attend to another task.

After the arrangements are all in place, Laney pushes her empty cart back toward the storage room.

"Wait up, Laney!" Bruce calls out as he catches up with her. "How're things going? I'd hoped to get away sooner to check on you, but I've been entertaining a group of important business executives all day. I'm free now, though, to volunteer my expert skills in boutonniere making."

Laney laughs. "Believe it or not, everything is done. I'm going home to spend the evening with my girls."

When they reach the storage room, Bruce opens the door for her. "Where's Hugh?"

"He's playing in a golf tournament. I was supposed to go with him to the dinner afterward, but considering how tense things are between us, I opted out." She navigates her cart into the storage room. "Besides, I want to get a good night's sleep. I plan to spend the day working at the shop tomorrow."

"I'm a do-it-yourself kinda guy if you need a hand with anything," Bruce offers.

"How are you with a paintbrush?" she asks, a smile tugging at her lips.

"I've done more than my share of painting."

Laney parks the cart in the corner and straightens, one hand on her lower back. "In that case, I may take you up on your offer. My equipment arrives from Charlotte on Monday. With your help, I can knock out the painting tomorrow ahead of the delivery."

"Then count me in."

After helping her clean up the storeroom, Bruce walks her to her car. They make a plan to meet at nine in the morning, and true to his word, he's waiting with two cups of coffee when she arrives at the shop.

They start in the showroom. Bruce brushes a coat of high gloss yellow-green paint on the front door while Laney rolls the interior walls cream.

"How was your evening?" Bruce asks as they work.

"Great! The girls and I ordered pizza and watched *27 Dresses*."

"Any drama from Hugh?"

"Nope. He wasn't home when we went to bed around eleven, but his car was in the driveway this morning. Let's not spoil the day by talking about Hugh."

Bruce smiles over at her. "Fine by me."

They have no shortage of things to discuss. When they finish the door and walls, they tackle the checkout counter together before moving to the back room. Laney paints while Bruce puts together the commercial shelving she purchased yesterday at Home Depot in Hope Springs.

Laney orders take-out cheeseburger platters from Ruthie's for their lunches. When they finish painting around five o'clock, Laney cleans up and Bruce goes next door to Delilah's Delights for pistachio gelato. Upon his return, they stand by the sunny window in the showroom to enjoy their refreshing treat.

"I enjoyed today. You're fun to hang out with, Laney," he says, rubbing a smudge of gelato from the corner of her mouth.

She removes his hand. "Bruce . . ."

"Don't worry. I'm not going to kiss you." He takes her empty cup and sets it with his on the checkout counter. "But I need to say this." He places his hands on her shoulders. "We have chemistry, Laney. I think you sense it too. But I would never make a move on you while you're with Hugh. All marriages have their difficulties. I'm a strong advocate for counseling. But sometimes there's nothing left to fight for. I work with Hugh. I've seen all sides of him, none of them good. You deserve to be happy, to be with someone who appreciates you. Whether that someone is me or another lucky guy, save yourself while you can." He kisses her cheek and disappears through the swinging door into the back room.

Laney's heart fills with warmth at the same time dread overcomes her. She's just crossed the line into forbidden territory.

She's still standing there, with a hand pressed to her cheek where Bruce kissed her, when Hugh bursts through the freshly painted front door. "You need to come with me. Dad has summoned us to Love-Struck for an important announcement."

"Go without me. I'm not in the mood for your family's drama."

Hugh looks down at the two empty gelato cups and back up at her. "I'm not asking you, Laney. I'm telling you."

CHAPTER 13
ADA

Ada has avoided Bud all week. She's visited Glory daily, but she's declined Bud's invitations for trail rides. She hopes that distancing herself from the situation will appease Stuart. Perhaps he'll come around, and over time, accept her.

Late Sunday afternoon, she and Enzo are at Primo Vino, unloading cases of wine and organizing them on the new shelves, when Stuart texts her an image. She enlarges the image and gasps at the sight of Stuart with one arm around Glory's neck and a syringe in his opposite hand. She's still staring at the pic when another message from him appears on the screen. *Disclaim your inheritance or else.*

"I gotta go. There's a problem with Glory," Ada says to Enzo as she retrieves her purse from the back office.

Enzo follows her to the door. "Do you want me to come with you?"

Ada hesitates. She very much wants him with her in case something drastic happens. But she's used to fighting her own battles, and for the sake of her self-esteem, she needs to stand up to Stuart herself.

She pecks his cheek. "You finish up here. I'm sure everything's fine. I just need to check on her."

Ten minutes later, Ada is pulling into the equestrian center when Siri announces a text message from Daniel Love. The message reads, *I'm summoning the family for a meeting at five o'clock today. I realize it's last minute, but I have important news to share that can't wait.*

Ada parks in front of the stable and thumbs off her response. *I'm no longer a member of the family, remember?*

Daniel texts back. *You will always be a part of the family. My news is devastating. I need you here for support.*

Devastating? Is he sick? Or broke? Or is this a ploy to get back in her good graces? She texts back. *I'm in the middle of something. I'll make it if I can.*

Ada enters the stable and is relieved to see Glory munching on hay in her stall, seemingly healthy and unscathed. The syringe is lying on the ground in front of her stall. She picks it up and examines it. Fortunately, there's no needle attached. It's a warning from Stuart intended to scare her.

Picking up the syringe, she turns to leave and runs straight into Bud. "Hello, Ada. It's nice to see you. I've missed riding with you this week."

Ada slips the syringe into her pocket before he sees it. "I've been busy at Primo Vino." She checks the time on the clock above the stalls. She has five minutes to make the ten-minute drive to Love-Struck. As much as she dreads seeing Daniel, curiosity can't keep her away. "I need to run. I have to be somewhere."

Bud follows her outside to her car. "You're avoiding me. You're upset about what happened with Stuart."

Ada lets out a sigh. She can't put him off forever. "I'm not upset with you, Bud. I've been trying to sort through some things. I'd like to talk to you about something, though. Are you free in the morning?"

"I plan to be here all day. Come whenever you can get away."

"I'll try to get here before noon," Ada says, slipping into her car and speeding off.

Ada is the last of the Love siblings to arrive at The Nest. Her half brothers and Casey are lined up on the velvet sofa in her father's wood-paneled library, the venue for all important family meetings. Laney is the only spouse in attendance, and she's seated in a wing chair looking uncomfortable, as though she'd rather be anywhere else than here.

Sheldon moves over to make room for Ada on the sofa, but she chooses the matching wing chair opposite Laney.

"Thank you all for coming on such short notice. I don't want to take up too much of your time on a Sunday evening." Daniel paces back and forth in front of them. "I hope you don't mind if I remain standing. What I'm about to tell you won't be easy."

Sheldon narrows his pale olive eyes, the same hue as their father's and Casey's. "You're scaring us, Dad. Whatever it is, just say it."

"All right then. I have stage four colon cancer."

A collective gasp spreads across the room. But everyone, including Ada, is too stunned to speak.

Daniel goes on, "Typically, metastasized colon cancer spreads to the liver and lungs. Unfortunately, mine has spread to my pancreas."

Ada knows enough about cancer to understand this is terrible news. She glances around the room. Her siblings are staring at the floor and wiping at their eyes. She appears to be the only one not crying.

Casey jumps to her feet and crosses the room to Daniel. Taking hold of his hands, she says, "We'll fight this! You're strong. You can beat it. I assume you've seen an oncologist. Is surgery an option?"

Daniel's lips part in a sad smile. "I've seen several oncologists. There are no options. I'll be lucky to make it until Christmas."

"No!" Casey sobs. "This can't be happening. I just lost my mother. I refuse to let you die too."

Daniel pulls her in for a half hug. "I'm sorry, sweetheart," he says, kissing the top of her head. "But you don't have any say in the matter. This is up to God."

He walks Casey back to her seat. "I've known about this long enough to accept my fate. I want to enjoy what little time I have left with the five of you." His eyes circle the room, landing on Ada.

"Can't they at least try chemo?" Sheldon asks. "And what about clinical trials?"

"They can try. But it won't work. Why would I put myself through a grueling regime of chemotherapy when I have so little time left?"

Hugh looks incredulously at him. "What're we supposed to do, just sit by and watch you die?"

"On the contrary. I have no intention of moping around. We're going to be busy. I have many goals to accomplish, and I need your help."

"What sort of goals?" Charles asks in a suspicious tone.

"We can talk about those later, once everyone has come to terms with my diagnosis. I'll be speaking with each of you individually in the coming days." Daniel walks over to the wet bar and fills a tumbler with brown liquid. "Now leave me in peace to enjoy my fifty-year-old scotch. I'm sure your significant others are waiting for you."

Everyone stands at once, eager to be alone with their thoughts. Ada is on her way out of the room when Daniel calls her back in. "Ada, may I have a word with you?"

She turns to face him, but she's too overcome with emotion to speak.

"Close the door and sit down," Daniel says in a stern voice.

Ada does as she's told. The years shed away, and she's thirteen years old again in trouble for lying to her mother about a poor grade.

Daniel sits down next to her at the end of the sofa. "I realize you and I aren't on the best of terms. And I have only myself to blame." He crosses his legs and sips his scotch. "I can't leave this earth until I've made things right with you. I very much want to see you married to Enzo. I hope you'll let me host your wedding. Walking you down the aisle is my dying wish."

Ada studies her father's face. He doesn't look sick. In fact, he's never looked healthier, fit and tan from hours spent on the tennis court. "I don't see how we can possibly make a wedding like that happen in such a short amount of time."

"Why not? We have everything we need at our disposal. We'll meet with the event planner tomorrow to see about our options for dates."

Ada stands to leave. "I can't make any promises until I talk to Enzo."

"Of course. Bring him along tomorrow if you'd like." Daniel walks her to the door. "I'll check everyone's schedule and text you some potential meeting times in the morning."

Ada flees the house as the first tears stream down her cheeks. The anger she's felt for Daniel for so long has vanished, replaced by a deep sorrow she's only known once before in her life—when her mother died suddenly from a brain aneurysm thirteen years ago.

She gets in her car, but instead of returning to town, she heads in the opposite direction. She drives aimlessly through the mountains, crying and screaming and pounding the steering wheel. How can this be happening? Daniel is so young, so vital, with so much living left to do. This will be his last Thanksgiving. He'll never get to meet her children, never again see the summer sun disappear beyond the horizon.

Enzo is waiting at home with a chilled bottle of pinot grigio and marinated chicken breasts, ready for the grill. "Have you been crying?" he asks when she enters the kitchen.

Ada grabs a napkin and wipes her eyes. "Wait until I tell you why." She declines his offer of wine. "I need something stronger."

He raises an eyebrow. "Stronger as in . . ."

"Tequila." She pours two fingers of Casa Dragones over ice and leans against the kitchen counter. "I've just learned Daniel has terminal cancer."

Enzo lets out a whistle. "Oh boy." He pauses a beat while the news sinks in. "This must be very confusing for you, considering what you've been through with Daniel these past months."

Ada shakes her glass, rattling her ice cubes. "Strange how none of that seems to matter now. All my animosity toward him evaporated into thin air," she says and drains the tequila.

Enzo lifts the platter of chicken breasts from the counter. "Let's start the grill. If you're going to drink tequila like that, we need to get some food in your stomach."

On the terrace, while they wait for the grill to heat, Ada fills him in on Daniel's prognosis and his desire to see her married before he dies. "I didn't know what to say to him. How can I deny a dying man his last request? He wants us to meet with the event planner tomorrow morning to see what dates are available. I know this is sudden, Enzo. And I totally understand if you'd rather wait. We can tell him together tomorrow."

"I have to work at Foxtail in the morning. But you know how I feel, Ada. I'll marry you anytime, anywhere. If this is what you want, I'm all for it," Enzo says, forking the chicken breasts onto the grill.

"That's just it, though. I'm not sure what I want. I was warming up to the idea of a small wedding."

Enzo lowers the grill's lid. "Then agree to a small-scale wedding at Love-Struck. If he truly wishes to make amends with you, he'll be willing to compromise."

Ada snorts. "Daniel Love doesn't compromise."

"Maybe not with other people. But you have the upper hand. Hold your ground, Ada. This is your wedding. You don't have to do anything you don't want to."

"That's easier said than done," Ada mumbles. Daniel can be very persuasive, and now that he has terminal cancer, how can she possibly refuse him anything? She's worked so hard to cut ties with Daniel. Now, in a blink of an eye, she's fallen back into his trap.

CHAPTER 14
DANIEL

The devastated faces of his children haunt Daniel throughout the evening. And that night, he dreams of his own funeral. The coffin is open, and he pretends to be asleep. Tears stream down their cheeks and land on his skin like electric jolts. Only his body is paralyzed, and he cannot reach out to them.

Daniel wakes at daybreak in a cold sweat. Having been preoccupied with getting Ada and Ruthie back, he's never considered the heartache his charade would bring his children. But the cat's out of the bag, and he can't stop now. After Ada's wedding, he'll fake enrollment in a clinical trial in a foreign country with advanced medical technology. He'll return home miraculously cured a month later, and no one will be the wiser.

Daniel foregoes breakfast and heads straight to his office. At eight o'clock, he's seated at his desk with his door open when Sonia passes by in the hall. She may lack experience, but she tries hard. Whether she actually has any brains remains to be seen.

He calls out to her, and she appears in the doorway. "Did you need to see me, sir?"

"Yes, come in. I have a personal matter to discuss with you." He motions her to the chair opposite his desk. "The doctors have diagnosed me with terminal pancreatic cancer." He omits the part about the cancer starting in his colon. The mention of pancreatic cancer is effective in getting people's attention.

Her face crumbles. "That's awful, Mr. Love. I'm so sorry."

"Yes . . . well . . . I'm trying not to dwell on it. I have much I want to accomplish before I die. On the top of that list is hosting my daughter's wedding."

Sonia's face lights up. "Seriously? That's so exciting. When did Casey and Luke get engaged?"

"I'm talking about Ada, not Casey. Time is of the essence. What Saturdays are free in the next couple of months?"

"I'll have to check the calendar, but we have at least two, maybe three, available weekends. I hope you're planning a small wedding. With so little time, there's no way we can possibly swing an enormous event on such short notice."

"That's not for you to decide. We'll bring Casey in on the planning if necessary. Let's meet in the conference room at ten. And don't forget to bring your calendar. Now run along." He shoos her away, and she scurries out of his office.

Over the course of the next hour, his children drop in, one by one, to express their deep sorrow at his unfortunate prognosis. He tells each of them the same thing. "I don't need your pity, and I don't want you fawning over me. Let's make the most of the time I have left."

Casey is the last to stop by. She's visibly upset, and her sad face brings him pangs of guilt.

"I can't believe this," she sobs. "Why is this happening when we're just getting to know each other?"

Daniel takes her in his arms. "I know, sweetheart. It doesn't seem fair. We've had so little time together. Let's concentrate on making memories you can cherish after I'm gone."

This only makes her cry harder, and she blubbers for several minutes before she finally settles down. "I need your help in planning Ada's wedding," Daniel says, holding her at arm's length.

"Maybe the two of you will become friends. You'll need to form an alliance against your brothers after I'm gone."

Casey stares at him with a blank face, and he can't tell what she's thinking. But when they meet in the conference room an hour later, she chooses a chair at the table next to Ada.

"Where's Enzo?" Daniel asks in a disappointed tone.

"He had to work," Ada says. "But he and I agree about our wishes for the wedding."

Daniel places his hands, one on top of the other, on the table. "In that case, let's discuss dates. I trust you brought the calendar, Sonia."

"Yes, sir." The event planner flips open her calendar. "We have two Saturdays available, one the last weekend in October and the other Thanksgiving."

Ada blurts, "It'll have to be Thanksgiving."

Daniel says, "Given the circumstances, I think sooner is better. We'll have a chance for more pleasant weather in October."

"But that's only a month away," Sonia objects, her blue eyes wide like a deer in the headlights.

Ada adds, "And everyone will think I'm pregnant."

A solemn expression falls over Daniel's face. "Everyone will know I'm deathly ill. My health will have deteriorated significantly by Thanksgiving. I might even be bedridden. October it is." He feels awful for lying. There's no way he can keep up this farce until Thanksgiving.

"With all due respect, Mr. Love, our calendar is booked. I can't add another thing to my plate right now. I'm—"

Daniel's steely glare shuts Sonia up. "I told you earlier, we're bringing Casey in to help. And, as you know, Ada was once our event planner. She did the job better than you ever will."

After an awkward moment of silence, Ada says, "I agree there's not enough time to organize a big wedding. Enzo and I would prefer a family-only ceremony in the chapel, followed by a small reception."

Sonia raises her hand. "I vote for smaller."

"As prominent members of local society, we have certain expectations to fulfill." Daniel flashes Ada his warmest smile. "And I want the whole town to watch us parade down the aisle on our big day." His gaze shifts to Casey. "We'll use the guest list from the Fourth of July party."

Ada's jaw drops to the table. "But there are over four hundred people on that list."

Daniel intertwines his fingers. "Then we'll compromise. We'll shave the list down to three hundred. We can't possibly ask fewer than that."

"Some compromise," Ada says under her breath. "The major considerations are invitations, entertainment, and my dress. I can probably find a sample gown, and I'm fine with hiring a deejay, but I refuse to send out e-vites for my wedding."

"My department can design the invitation for you," Casey says. "We'll hand-deliver them if necessary."

"We'll all pitch in with the planning." Daniel nudges Ada's arm. "I have an idea. Why don't you and I fly to New York at the end of the week to shop for your wedding dress? We can stay at the Ritz-Carlton and eat at our favorite restaurants."

Out of the corner of his eye, Daniel notices Casey's smile fade as she lowers her gaze. Everyone is so emotional today. Things were a lot less complicated when they were all mad at him.

"I'll figure out my dress if I decide to go through with the wedding." Ada pushes back from the table. "I appreciate what you're trying to do, Daniel. But I'm feeling overwhelmed. Give me the afternoon to think about it. I'll be in touch," she says, and hurries out of the conference room before he can stop her.

Sonia gathers her things. "Excuse me. I need to make some calls," she says and slips out.

Daniel reaches across the table for Casey's hand. "Are you okay, sweetheart? You seemed sad when I mentioned New York. Did it bring back painful memories of losing your mother?"

"That's not it at all. Hearing you talk about shopping trips with Ada reminds me of how much you and I have missed out on.

But we can't erase the past." Casey stands abruptly. "I'm going to catch up with Ada. She seems like she could use a friend right now."

Casey has no sooner left the conference room when his phone vibrates the table with a call from Ruthie. In a tearful voice, she asks, "Is it true? Are you really dying?"

He settles back in his chair, a Cheshire cat grin spreading across his lips. "News travels fast."

"It appears your event planner can't keep a secret," Ruthie says. "She told a woman in accounting who told one of my wait-staff when she came in for a breakfast meeting."

Daniel isn't surprised. Sonia is not only inexperienced, she's immature. "There's no way to keep something like this a secret."

"Isn't there anything the doctors can do?"

"Unfortunately, no."

"Oh, Daniel. I don't know what to say. You're so young. This isn't fair."

"Life isn't fair, Ruthie," Daniel says, choking back a sob. What he's doing to his loved ones is so awful, an all-time low for him.

"Come over tonight. Let me cook dinner for you."

"That'd be nice," he says with a sniffle.

If Daniel could turn back the clock, he never would have set this scam into motion. But since he can't change things, he might as well make the most of it.

CHAPTER 15
ADA

Ada flees the building to the safety of her car. She's backing out of the parking space when Casey appears at the passenger window.

Ada puts the car in park and rolls down the window. "My head is spinning. Did I just get shanghaied into a large wedding?"

Casey sticks her head into the car. "Daniel tried to shanghai you, but you stood your ground. You haven't committed to anything yet. Don't let him bully you, Ada. I have a feeling he'll concede to a small wedding."

Ada stares down at her steering wheel. "I shouldn't let him get under my skin. Especially when he's . . ." Her voice trails off as tears well in her eyes.

"I know you're overwhelmed, and I'm happy to help. If you need to bounce ideas off of me or want me to go wedding dress shopping with you. Maybe someplace closer than New York."

Ada looks up at her. "Thanks. That means a lot coming from you."

An impish smile crosses Casey's lips. "Does this mean we're friends?"

Ada laughs. "It means we're entering friendly territory. We're far from being besties."

"I consider that progress," Casey says, stepping away from the car.

The tension eases from Ada's body as she drives off. After everything that's transpired between them, is it possible she and Casey could become friends? Ada certainly hopes so. She could use a friend right now.

When she arrives at the equestrian center and parks her car at the stable, Bud is standing at the arena railing, staring at a spot off in the distance. He's so preoccupied, he doesn't acknowledge her presence.

She sidles up to him and says, "Are you okay, Bud?"

He startles, his hand gripping his chest. "Ada! I didn't hear you." He angles his body toward her. "I just heard some distressing news. It's about Daniel. I'm not sure if it's true."

Ada sighs. "It's true. He broke the news to us last night. How'd you find out?"

"Ruthie overheard one of her customers, a staffer at Love-Struck. Daniel and I have had our differences in the past, but I would never wish this fate on my worst enemy. How's he handling it?"

"Surprisingly well. He's determined to make the most of the time he has left. That includes hosting my wedding at Love-Struck."

His face falls. "I see."

"It's been a stressful morning. Any chance I could trouble you for a cup of your lavender tea?"

"Of course. Let's go inside." He steps aside, motioning for her to walk ahead of him.

When they reach the house, they cross the porch and enter the open french doors to the kitchen. Ada takes a seat at the counter, watching as Bud fills the tea kettle and places it on the stove. He is the only man she knows who drinks hot tea, let alone makes his own special brew. But his is the best she's ever tasted and works wonders at calming her nerves.

Ada plants her elbows on the table and clasps her hands

together. "I haven't forgotten about your generous offer to host my wedding. But I'm feeling caught in the middle. Ever since I was a small girl, Daniel and I have dreamed about my wedding day." She snickers. "I no longer care about that fairytale. But it seems so important to him. I don't know how I can turn him down."

Bud scoops loose tea into two stainless steel pods and places the pods in mugs. "This is your wedding, Ada. Don't let Daniel use his disease to coerce you into anything you aren't ready for."

"I'm totally ready to get married. I've been thinking a lot lately about what kind of wedding I want. Having three hundred virtual strangers witness my most intimate moment seems intrusive. Enzo wants to elope to a tropical destination. I was against the idea at first. But now it seems so reasonable, a wedding and a honeymoon all tied into one neat package."

"An elopement would certainly solve your problem with Daniel," Bud says, returning the kettle to the stove.

"We'll see. I'm hoping he'll agree to scale down the guest list. I haven't agreed to anything yet."

"If you decide to go through with it, just make sure I'm on the guest list," Bud says, wagging his finger at her.

She smiles at him. "I will, for sure."

When the tea finishes steeping, they take their mugs outside to the rockers on the porch. They sit for a minute in silence. "I'm sorry, Bud. But with planning a wedding and opening the wine shop, now is not the best time for me to commit to working for you."

"I totally understand, and I'll manage fine on my own. I mainly wanted to show you the ropes in case something happens to me. Which doesn't seem such a far-fetched idea given Daniel's diagnosis."

"Nothing is going to happen to you." Ada inhales a deep breath. "But since you mentioned it, I'd like for you to remove me from your will as heir to the farm. Everything has happened so fast. Maybe we can revisit the issue in a few years when we're more comfortable with our new family dynamics."

"If you're sure that's what you want," Bud says without hesitation.

"It's best for everyone involved," Ada responds, even though it's not at all what she wants. It's what Stuart wants. Ada had anticipated more pushback from Bud, even had her argument ready.

An awkward silence settles over the porch while they drink their tea. Finally, Ada stands. "I should go. Enzo and I need to decide about this wedding."

Bud remains seated. "Don't be a stranger."

"I won't." After returning her cup to the kitchen, she hurries away from the house, feeling as though she's leaving a piece of her heart behind.

———

Ada is surprised to find Sheldon's pickup truck in Enzo's driveway. When she enters the house, loud voices draw her to the kitchen where Enzo and Sheldon are cooking fajitas. She stands in the doorway watching Sheldon slice peppers while Enzo cooks chicken in a grill pan on the stove. They've grown closer since Enzo's been working for Ollie. Watching them now, they seem like old friends.

Ada drops her bag on the counter and hugs Enzo from behind. "I thought you had to work."

Enzo cranes his neck to kiss the top of her head. "I finished early, and Sheldon wanted to see the wine shop."

"And then I got hungry, so here we are." Sheldon hunches his shoulders up to his ears like a naughty little boy feigning innocence.

Ada pokes her brother in his belly. "You're always hungry."

"It's worse since now that we're eating for two," he says, crunching a slice of yellow pepper.

Ada rolls her eyes. "You're ridiculous. When did you learn to cook?"

"Since I married Ollie. She's a disaster in the kitchen." Sheldon wipes his hand on a towel. "I enjoy your fiancé's company. I approve of your marriage."

Ada rests her head on Enzo's shoulder. "Did you hear that? Sheldon approves of us. We can get married now."

"I heard," Enzo says, flipping the chicken breasts over. "Speaking of weddings, how was the meeting with Daniel?"

Dropping her arms from his waist, Ada retrieves a lemon LaCroix from the refrigerator and sits down at the counter. "There are two dates available. I lobbied for Thanksgiving weekend, and he insisted on the end of October. He agreed to reduce the guest list to three hundred, but that still seems huge to me. I told him I needed to think about it. I'm still not convinced this is the right thing for us."

Sheldon tosses his sliced vegetables in a saute pan. "I missed something. I thought you two were waiting a year to get married."

"We've been talking about moving the wedding up. Obviously, we'd like to do it on our terms, not Daniel's," Ada says and explains about their father's dying wish.

Sheldon turns off the heat, slides the pan to the back of the stove, and comes around to Ada's side of the island. "I used lunch as an excuse to come over and check on you. I admit, I can't believe Dad invited you to the meeting yesterday, after the way he's been treating you."

"He's had a change of heart. He wants me back in his life." A thought occurs to Ada. "Which makes perfect sense now that I think about it. He's atoning for his sins. With terminal cancer, he must be wondering where he'll land in the afterlife."

"So your forgiveness is his ticket to heaven," Enzo says, placing a platter of fajitas and three plates on the counter in front of them.

"Something like that," Ada says.

Sheldon reaches for a flour tortilla. "In his defense, discovering you're not his biological daughter has been hard on Dad. Although, I agree, he had a funny way of showing it. He wants you back because he loves and misses you."

"Ha. He wants me back because he's jealous of Bud. He can't stand for anyone else to be my father."

Sheldon adds chicken and vegetables to his tortilla, rolls it up, and takes a bite. With his mouth full, he says, "You must feel like a yo-yo being pulled in so many directions."

"You have no idea. Bud and I were just figuring out how we fit into each other's life when . . . Never mind." Her relationship with her father is none of Sheldon's business.

Sheldon gobbles down his fajita and reaches for another tortilla. "This wedding could be a great thing for Dad. The planning will occupy his mind, and the event itself will bring the whole family together one last time."

"Geez, Sheldon. Do you have to be so morbid?"

"I can't help it," Sheldon says. "The situation is morbid."

Ada eyes the plate of food, but she has no appetite for fajitas. She slides off her stool and goes to the refrigerator for a container of blueberry yogurt. Standing across the counter from them, she says, "You're quiet, Enzo. What do you think of all this?"

He looks up from his plate. "I've already told you. I'll marry you anytime, anywhere."

Ada drags her spoon around the yogurt container. "I'll go along with it, if Daniel will agree to a small, informal affair."

"That'll never happen," Sheldon says. "You know how Dad loves to throw a party. There are worse things than being a princess for a day."

She glares at him. "Easy for you to say. You don't have to be the major attraction at the circus."

"What are you talking about? I just got married two weeks ago." Sheldon lifts his left hand, showing off his wedding band.

"It's different when you're the bride." Ada slams the yogurt container down on the counter. "All right! I'll do it! But only because I'll feel guilty for the rest of my life if I don't."

Sheldon's expression is solemn. "That's true. You will."

"Are you sure you're okay with this?" she asks Enzo.

"Absolutely," Enzo says. "I'm great with this. All I care about is being married to you."

Ada blows him an air kiss. "You and I are going somewhere far away with white sandy beaches and plenty of glorious sunshine on our honeymoon."

Enzo beams. "Now you're talking."

"Looks like I'm going to Washington, wedding dress shopping, tomorrow."

"I'll go with you," Enzo volunteers.

"No, you won't either. You can't see my dress until our wedding day. I'll get Casey to go with me, since she volunteered." Ada grabs her phone and thumbs off a text to Casey.

"Yes," Sheldon says, punching the air. "I knew the two of you would one day become friends. Dad will be thrilled."

"I'm not doing it for Daniel. I'm doing it for me."

CHAPTER 16
LANEY

Laney walks through the shop one last time before locking up for the day. The space, with the addition of refrigeration units and display fixtures, is looking like a legitimate business.

She's getting in her car when Sonia calls in a panic. "You will not believe this. Sylvia has defaulted on all her wedding contracts. She claims her social life is suddenly too busy for her to do wedding flowers, but you and I both know it's because you quit on her. Please, tell me you can take over."

"Absolutely," Laney says without hesitation. "I'm grateful for the business. You can count on me. I promise I won't let you down."

Sonia lets out an audible sigh of relief. "Those are the words I needed to hear. Let's meet first thing in the morning to go over the contracts."

"Sounds good. I'll be at Love-Struck at nine."

As she heads off to the grocery store, Laney mentally calculates the money she stands to make on the weddings. With this unexpected extra income, she'll soon be able to hire an assistant. She's postponing her grand opening until she's ready for regular store hours. That time might be sooner than expected.

Laney picks up a few items for dinner at the market and continues home. She's carrying her grocery bags to the kitchen when she spots Hugh talking on the phone on the terrace, pacing with a tumbler of whiskey in hand. On closer inspection, she realizes he's not on the phone. He's talking to himself.

After returning home from Love-Struck last night, Hugh had gotten drunk and cried like a baby over his father's cancer diagnosis. When she attempted to console him, he'd mistaken her sympathy for affection and tried to seduce her. She'd fought him off and locked herself in the guest room. They haven't spoken since.

Laney puts away her groceries and begins working on dinner. She's cooking shredded chicken for tacos when Hugh comes in from outside. She braces herself for his wrath, but he's surprisingly cheerful.

"Let's grab the girls and go to the club for dinner," Hugh says, refilling his tumbler with ice.

Laney gestures at the pan with her wooden spoon. "But I've already started the tacos." She has no interest in going out to dinner with him, and she doesn't want to give him false hope about their marriage.

"Why not save it until tomorrow night?"

"Sorry. But the girls will be ravished when they get home from practice. And I'm sure they'll have homework. I'm glad to see you're in a better mood, though."

Hugh pours whiskey over his ice. "I'm trying to look at the bright side of the situation."

"Good for you. What is the bright side?"

"When Dad dies, I'll inherit one-fourth of his shares of Love-Struck stock. Since I already bought Ada's interest, I'll be the majority shareholder."

"Better not let your father hear you talking like this," Laney says, stirring in a package of taco seasoning and adding the recommended amount of water.

"You don't get it, Laney. This will have an enormous impact on our lives. I'll be making way more money. We can buy that bigger house you've been dreaming about."

Laney turns the stove off and faces him. "I don't dream of bigger homes, Hugh. I dream of happy ones. Your father's diagnosis changes nothing. Our marriage is still in trouble."

"I'm working on that." Hugh gives her his little boy innocent look, which no longer works on her.

"We need marriage counseling, not dinner at the club."

"You know how I feel about that subject." Hugh drains his whiskey. "I despise tacos. I'm going to the club for dinner without you."

She eyes his empty glass. "You've been drinking. How're you getting there?"

"Chester's picking me up. We're meeting the others at the club. My friends heard about Dad, and they want to comfort me. At least someone cares about me."

She narrows her eyes at him. "Why did you ask me to dinner when you already have plans?"

"Because I knew you'd say no." He pinches her cheek hard. "You're predictable, Laney. Boring as hell."

A car horn sounds from outside. "There's Chester now." Hugh turns toward the hall. "Don't wait up for me."

She calls after him. "Don't worry. I won't."

Laney, vowing not to let him get to her, returns to her meal preparation. She has all the taco fixings on a platter when the girls arrive home fifteen minutes later from field hockey practice. As predicted, her daughters are starving and scarf down their dinner. She asks them about their day, but they're cranky and say little.

Now that they're getting older, her girls are growing apart from her. Laney isn't resentful about this natural progression like some parents. She's grateful they're well-adjusted kids—straight A students with plenty of friends. Although taking care of them once occupied much of her time and their absence has left a void in her life, she's blessed to have discovered a new career to fill the vacuum.

After cleaning up from dinner, Laney pours herself a glass of pinot noir and goes to her desk where she spends an hour pinning images of arrangements to Pinterest boards to help brides identify styles of flowers for their weddings.

Laney retires to the guest room around nine. Changing into her pajamas, she climbs into bed and calls Bruce. Even though they talk on the phone every night, they never run out of things to say. When they find themselves on opposite sides of an issue, they respectfully agree to disagree. Tonight, their conversation lasts for over two hours. She tells him how the shop is shaping up, and about Sylvia defaulting on her wedding contracts. And he talks about the progress he's made revamping the vineyard's varietals.

Laney feels like a teenager again, whispering into the phone so her parents can't hear her in the next room. Where's the harm in having romantic feelings for him if she doesn't act on them?

At eleven o'clock, the front door slams shut, and feet pound the stairs. "Laney!" Hugh bellows from outside her room.

Laney whispers to Bruce, "Hugh's home. I've gotta go." She jabs at the end call button and tosses the phone on the bed.

Hugh bangs on the door. "Open this damn door right now."

Swinging her legs over the side of the bed, she goes to the door and cracks it open an inch. "Be quiet! The girls are asleep."

He staggers into the door, forcing it open wider. "This is my house, and I'll talk as loud as I damn well want," he says, his voice growing even more shrill. "You're my wife, and I'm tired of you depriving me of sex." Grabbing a handful of her hair, he pulls her face close and presses his mouth to hers. He tastes like whiskey and cigars.

Laney gags and shoves him away. "Get off of me," she says in an angry whisper.

He paws at her pajama top. "Bitch, I need to get laid. Shut your mouth, and open your legs."

"Are you crazy? The girls can hear you." Over his shoulder, Grace appears in her bedroom doorway. "Grace is watching you."

When he turns to look at Grace, Laney shoves him out of the

room and locks the door. She slips back into bed, pulling the covers beneath her chin. When she hears someone calling her name, she takes a few seconds to realize it's Bruce on her phone.

She pats the covers until she finds her phone. "Bruce! Are you still there? I thought I disconnected the call."

"You must have missed the end button, because I heard everything Hugh said just now. He verbally assaulted you, Laney. He threatened to rape you. You're in imminent danger."

"You're overreacting. Hugh is a bully, but he's not a rapist."

"He's out of his mind, drunk. No telling what he might do."

"Hold on a second." She slides the phone beneath her pillow and goes to the door, pressing her ear against it. When she hears nothing, she peeks out into the hall. The other bedroom doors are all closed.

Retrieving her phone, she slips beneath the covers. "He's gone to bed."

"Still, I'm staying on the phone with you until you're sure."

"If you insist," Laney says, turning off her lamp.

Laney, comforted by the dark, pours her soul out to Bruce about how desperately unhappy she is in her marriage.

"You have to leave him, Laney."

"I can't now, not until after . . ." She catches herself. "Not while his father is ill."

"The timing will be even worse after Daniel dies. Hugh will be in mourning, and your guilt will prevent you from leaving him. You'd need to get out now, Laney. Before something terrible happens."

"Maybe you're right. But in a few weeks. I'm a business owner now. I have to think about my reputation. My customers will think I'm a horrible person if I abandon my husband in his time of need."

Bruce's breath is heavy on the other end. "I understand your point. But I hope your sacrifice doesn't cost you your life."

CHAPTER 17
DANIEL

Daniel arrives at Ruthie's promptly at six thirty with a bottle of bubbles and a bouquet of roses cut from his garden. Instead of hiding his car in the garage, he parks on the street, marches up to the front door, and rings the bell.

Ruthie looks amazing in cropped jeans and a pink silk top with her blonde hair brushing her shoulders the way he likes it. She takes him in her arms and hugs him tight. No words are needed. This is her way of expressing her sorrow over his terminal condition.

The feel of her body drives him mad with desire, and he pushes her gently away. "Sorry. The thorns are pricking me."

"Oops." She takes the flowers from him. "These are gorgeous. I'll put them in some water."

He follows her into the kitchen, and while she locates a vase, he pops the cork on the champagne and fills two glasses.

"This hardly seems like an occasion to celebrate," she says when he hands her a glass.

He touches the tip of his finger to the end of her nose. "Since when does the Queen of Bubbles need a special occasion to drink champagne?"

Ruthie giggles. "Since never. You're in an awfully good mood for someone . . ." Rosy spots appear on her cheeks. "You know, considering the circumstances."

Daniel shrugs. "There's no point in dwelling on my misfortune. I want to enjoy every minute I have left. And I'd like to do that with you, if you'll take me back."

Ruthie turns away from him. "We need to have a serious discussion before I agree to anything. But we can talk while we eat." Setting her champagne glass on the counter, she opens the oven and removes a casserole dish. "The lasagna's ready. Do you mind getting the salad out of the refrigerator?"

Minutes later, they are seated at the small round table on her screened porch. He patiently answers the same questions his children asked about his condition. He experiences a pang of guilt with each lie that crosses his lips. The more lies he tells, the more lies he invents to cover his tracks.

He eats the last bite of lasagna and wipes his mouth with a pink linen napkin. "Can we stop talking about my cancer and have that discussion about us?"

"I can't go back to the way things were, Daniel. I need more."

Daniel's expression tightens. "I hardly see the point of getting married when I only have a few months left to live."

"I'm hoping you have longer than a few months." She pushes her plate away. "And I'm not talking about marriage. I want to go public with our relationship."

Daniel thinks back to the night of the Coleman wedding. Ruthie had looked so elegant in her emerald-green dress. Hands down, she's the best-looking woman her age he knows. And everyone in town thinks highly of her. He insisted on keeping their relationship secret in case someone better came along. Someone with a more distinguished pedigree. And that woman had come along. What a loser Caroline Horton turned out to be.

Placing both hands on the table, he leans toward her. "Then let's do it. We'll become a proper couple. You can be my date to Ada's wedding."

Ruthie moves to the edge of her chair. "Do you really mean it,

Daniel? You're willing to be exclusive? No more one-night stands?"

"No more one-night stands for me"—he thumbs his chest and then points at her—"if *you* promise not to go out with Bud again."

"That's an easy promise. I like Bud. He's laid back and fun to be with. But there were no sparks between us." She walks her fingers up Daniel's arm. "Not like the chemistry you and I have."

He brings her hand to his lips, nibbling on the tips of her fingers. "I've missed that chemistry. What say we seal this deal in bed?"

"Later." She snatches her hand away and jumps to her feet. "First, we're going to walk down Magnolia Avenue. I want the whole town to see me on your arm. Besides, I have a hankering for Delilah's gelato."

They quickly clean up from dinner and head out hand in hand toward the center of town. The night autumn air is cool, and when Ruthie shivers, Daniel pulls her close. "This is nice. I like being official."

"I told you," Ruthie says, placing an arm around his waist. "We should have done it a long time ago."

"We're doing it now. That's what counts."

Heads turn as they stroll down Magnolia Avenue. Ruthie whispers, "Look! People are staring at us. They're shocked to see the legendary bachelor, Daniel Love, on a date with a woman."

"They're not looking at me. They're thinking how pretty you are." Daniel's words sound corny to his ears, but he means them.

When they reach Delilah's Delights, they purchase two cups of coffee gelato and locate a table on the deck out back.

"So," Ruthie says, licking gelato off her plastic spoon. "Do you have a bucket list?"

"Besides Ada's wedding, I'm starting a couple of construction projects, and I hope to launch at least one of the new varietals. Bruce has promised a new Petit Verdot for the wedding."

"What do you think about us planning a trip for after the

wedding? You can pick the place, somewhere you've always wanted to go."

"I'm not much of a traveler. I have all the beautiful scenery I need right here in the mountains of Virginia." Seeing her disappointment, he adds, "But I'd love to take a trip with you. You can pick the place."

By then, Daniel will supposedly be on his way to Spain or India for his clinical trial. He'll disappear for six or eight weeks to a remote place like the Aleutian Islands in Alaska where no one will ever find him. He imagines the teary reunion when he returns home for Christmas, magically cured. His children and their new wives and husbands will gather around his dining room table for a feast fit for a king on Christmas Eve. He'll buy them lavish gifts. Fly-fishing gear for Sheldon. A new horse for Ada. Maybe even a diamond engagement ring for Ruthie.

"Hello? Anybody in there?" Ruthie says, stabbing him with her plastic spoon.

"Sorry. I have a lot on my mind these days."

Ruthie's smile fades. "Of course, you do."

Her sad face tugs at his heartstrings. Daniel will rot in hell for putting his loved ones through this. But his charade is working. Ada and Ruthie are back in his life. When this is all over, he'll make it up to them.

He reaches for her hand. "What were you saying?"

"That I've always wanted to drive down the West Coast, starting in the Olympic National Park and ending in San Diego."

"That sounds perfect. We'll rent a luxury convertible, and stay in the most luxurious hotels, and dine in the best restaurants."

He vows to one day take her on this trip. Maybe next spring or summer. Maybe even for their honeymoon.

CHAPTER 18
ADA

Ada spends a sleepless night, worrying that her car ride to DC with Casey will be awkward. But before they exit the town limits, Casey is chattering about her new condo and budding romance with Luke as though they are old friends.

Casey twirls a strand of her golden hair around her finger. "Luke is older than me, and he's ready for a more serious relationship. But I've had so many changes in my life this past year, I'd like to take things a little slower."

Ada gives her a knowing nod. "I felt that way, too, when Enzo and I first got engaged. We hadn't been together long, and I thought we were rushing things. Now I can't wait to be his wife and start our life together."

Casey drops her smile. "Daniel's diagnosis is a lesson for us all to live each day to the fullest. I can't believe he's dying. It seems so surreal."

"I haven't fully wrapped my mind around it yet," Ada says as she merges onto the highway. "Losing your biological father when you're just getting to know him must be difficult for you."

"Not as difficult as it must be for you when he's been your father all your life."

Ada tightens her grip on the steering wheel. "My feelings for Daniel have been all over the place these past few months. I would have eventually forgiven him for the way he treated me. But now that I'm having to speed up the process, to force that forgiveness, my emotions are even more conflicted. I'm trying to put the hurt feelings aside. Some days are easier than others."

"I can't even imagine." Casey rummages through her bag for her sunglasses, cleaning them with the hem of her blouse before putting them on. "Daniel is thrilled to be hosting your dream wedding. His face lights up every time he talks about it."

"All little girls dream of fairy-tale weddings, Casey. Few rarely come true. Enzo wanted to elope, and I was coming around to the idea." A faraway look shines in her eyes. "I can see the two of us alone with our celebrant on the end of a long pier, surrounded by blue sky and turquoise water."

Casey smiles her approval. "That sounds heavenly. And so personal. Can you plan a tropical vacation for your honeymoon?"

"Unfortunately, the tropics will have to wait. We had a realistic discussion about our honeymoon last night. We're closing on our new house in mid-October. The painters will be working the two weeks before the wedding. As of now, we'll spend our wedding night at the Inn at Hope Springs, and then return to Lovely on Sunday to move."

"So not the dream wedding or dream honeymoon, but the dream house."

Ada laughs. "Exactly."

Casey removes a file from her work tote. "Since we have plenty of time on our hands, we might as well work on the wedding plans."

Ada's brow shoots up above her sunglass frames. "Isn't that Sonia's job? I've scheduled a meeting with her for Friday."

"My department is helping Sonia until we hire an assistant. She's a hard worker with loads of fresh ideas, but she's overwhelmed by the volume of weddings." Casey grins at Ada.

"Turns out we need two people to do the job you did so effortlessly."

"She'll get the hang of it. After a while, the weddings plan themselves."

"I'm not sure I believe that. Anyway, I'm interviewing an older woman at the end of the week. Millie has twenty-three years of experience planning events for the Country Club of Virginia in Richmond. She just moved to Lovely to be near her daughter and grandchildren."

"She sounds ideal. You'd better snatch her up before someone else does."

"Don't worry. We will." Casey removes her pen cap. "So, how many bridesmaids and groomsmen are you having?"

"None, as of now. Enzo only moved to town a few months ago. His parents are dead, and the rest of his family lives in Italy. As for bridesmaids, I could ask my sisters-in-law, but I'm not close to any of them."

"You at least need a maid or matron of honor and a best man."

"Are you volunteering for the job?" Ada asks, mischief tugging at her lips.

"Sure! I'd love to be your maid of honor. But that would mean we'd have to be friends."

"Last I checked, women don't invite their enemies to go wedding dress shopping."

"Unless they are helping plan your wedding." Casey shifts in her seat. "You had a right to be upset when I appeared from nowhere and disrupted your life. But it's not my fault your father slept with my mother. Anymore than it's your fault your mother slept with Bud. I'm ready to put this all behind us. I admire you, Ada. I think you're a total badass. And I'd very much like to be your friend."

Ada glances over at her. "Do you really think I'm a badass?"

"Um, ye-ah. You stand up for yourself, and you're comfortable in your own skin."

"You give me more credit than I deserve. But I appreciate the compliment." Ada smiles as she returns her attention to the road. "I'd be honored to have you as my maid of honor."

"Yay! That's settled. I assume you'll want Laney to do your flowers."

"Laney? What happened to Sylvia?"

"Didn't you hear? Laney and Sylvia had a falling out. Laney's opened her own shop on Magnolia Avenue, in the building between Ruthie's Diner and Delilah's Delights."

"Good for her! Laney has excellent taste, and she works hard. I'm sure she'll be a success," Ada says, and for the rest of the drive, they discuss flowers, color schemes, and bridesmaids' dresses.

As they're approaching the outskirts of Washington, Casey asks, "Do you know where we're going? I understand there are several bridal boutiques in DC."

"There's one boutique I'm particularly interested in. Bella's Bridal Boutique in Georgetown has the largest selection of sample gowns. We have an eleven o'clock appointment with Wendy, the sales associate I spoke with on the phone yesterday." Ada accesses her GPS on her dashboard computer screen and clicks on the address she had previously entered for the boutique. She follows the automated voice directions to the location.

Wendy greets them at the door. She gives Ada the once-over. "Your tall and lean figure will provide plenty of options. What style of dress did you have in mind?"

"Simple," Ada says.

Wendy chuckles. "Everyone's idea of simple is different." She starts off across the boutique, waving for Ada to follow. "I've already pulled a few in your size. The rack is waiting in the dressing room."

Ada looks over at Casey. "Are you coming with me?"

"You go ahead. I'll wait here." Casey grabs a bridal magazine off the coffee table in the salon and plops down on the white leather sofa. "Be sure to model the ones you like."

In the dressing room, Ada strips down to her underwear and

steps into the first gown. She stares in the mirror, angling her body one way and another. "It's pretty, but I don't want strapless."

"Okay, then. No strapless," Wendy says, unzipping the dress.

Ada tries on four more before she finds a minimalist dress with spaghetti straps. The champagne silk clings to her curves, making her feel not like a fairy-tale bride but a goddess.

Wendy stands beside her, scrutinizing her reflection in the mirror. "The fit is perfect, even the hem. Not everyone can pull off this dress. But it suits your sophisticated good looks. Do you want to show it to your friend?"

"Sure." When Ada emerges from the dressing room, Casey's pale eyes widen, and her mouth forms an O. "It's fabulous."

Ada twirls around. "Do you really think so?"

"Absolutely! Enzo will lose his mind when he sees you in that."

Uncertainty crosses Ada's face. "But it has spaghetti straps, and at the end of October, we might have a chilly day."

"I have just the thing." Wendy crosses the salon to a rack of wraps. She flips through them until she finds the one she's looking for—a cream-colored fake fur shrug with a high neck that fastens at the throat.

Ada slips on the shrug and walks over to a mirror. "I love it." Her eyes pop when she sees the price tag. "That's a lot of money for a fake."

"It's a good fake," Wendy says, running her hand across the soft fur.

"The entire ensemble is so you." Casey hands Wendy a credit card. "We'll take the shrug and the dress. It's on Daniel, Ada. He insisted you get whatever you want."

"No, Casey! I can't let him do that."

Casey cocks her head to the side. "Why not? Would you buy this dress if you were eloping with Enzo?"

Ada ponders her question. "I get your point."

So as not to cause a scene, Ada reluctantly agrees to let Daniel pay for the dress. But thirty minutes later, over mimosas at Farmers Fishers Bakers, she says, "I'm not sure I can do this, Casey. I'm still so angry at Daniel. Nothing about this wedding feels right."

"Given the circumstances, we can't wait until it feels right." Casey places her hand on top of Ada's. "He's dying, Ada. He may not make it to Christmas. All he wants is to walk you down the aisle."

Tears blur Ada's vision as reality hits home. For the first time, she allows herself to contemplate her father's fate. She imagines him ghost white and emaciated, with morphine dripping into his veins from an IV stand beside the bed. Daniel Love, her larger-than-life father, wasting away from cancer.

Ada blinks her tears away and sits up straight. "You're right. I should be flattered, and I'm acting like a spoiled brat. Who cares what kind of wedding I have? The important thing is, I'm marrying Enzo."

Casey squeezes her hand. "We'll make it fun. I promise."

The server brings their sushi rolls with an order of tuna tartare to share.

"Let's talk about what it'll take for you to be comfortable with this wedding," Casey says as they eat.

Ada drags a chip through the tuna tartare. "Well, I admit I'm excited about getting married at Love-Struck. I grew up there. The vineyard is my home. I'd just like a super scaled-down version of what Daniel has in mind."

"Instead of a ten-piece dance band, you could hire Luke's jazz ensemble," Casey suggests.

"Yes!" Ada comes out of her seat a little. "That's a brilliant idea. I love Twilight Groove."

"Good. I'll see if they're available." Casey dips a sushi roll into soy sauce. "We'll keep the food simple."

"Right. I was thinking of three stations. Tenderloin, shrimp and grits, and a raw seafood bar. And no champagne fountain."

"But champagne available at the bar," Casey says. "My department is in charge of the invitations. We'll send them to Daniel's A-list of people and scratch everyone else. Which will reduce the number of guests to about two fifty. I doubt he'll even notice. Even if he does, it'll be too late to do anything about it."

Ada narrows her eyes. "That seems kinda devious."

"He's done worse things," Casey says with a shrug. "We just made the major decisions. The rest will be a piece of cake."

"Thank goodness," Ada says in a tone of relief. "I have enough to worry about with the new house and wine shop opening next week."

"Ooh. Can I come?"

Ada touches her mimosa glass to Casey's. "You'd better. After all, you're my new best friend."

CHAPTER 19
LANEY

Hugh's behavior grows more belligerent by the day, his exuberance over his forthcoming inheritance a thing of the past. He pounds on her bedroom door late at night, calling her vulgar names and berating her for refusing to sleep with him. She's embarrassed for him. The girls hear everything he says. But Laney is powerless to stop him. If she comes out of her room, she fears he'll attack her.

His drunken tirade lasts longer than usual on Thursday night. He rants and raves until after midnight when he finally retreats to his bedroom. Thirty minutes later, Laney is whispering to Bruce on the phone when there's a light tapping on her door.

"I have to go. Someone's at the door. It must be one of the girls." Laney hangs up on Bruce and goes to the door. Grace is standing in the hallway with tears streaming down her face.

"Oh, honey. Come in." Laney takes her by the hand and pulls her into the room, locking the door behind them.

"I'm scared, Mom. I don't understand why you don't just divorce him. You've been sleeping in the guest room for over a year."

"It's complicated." Laney leads her daughter over to the bed, and they sit side by side on the edge of the mattress. "I'd hoped your father and I could work things out, but he refuses to go for counseling. Things have gotten so bad, I don't see any way to save the marriage."

Grace snatches a tissue from the box on the nightstand and swipes at her eyes. "Good! You've accepted it's over. Now kick him out of the house before he hurts you. Or us. Some of my friends' parents are divorced. It's not that big a deal."

"The problem is the timing." Laney angles her body toward Grace. "Your father received some devastating news on Sunday. Your grandfather has cancer, sweetheart."

Grace clamps her hand over her mouth. "Oh no! Poor Granddaddy. Is it bad?"

"I'm afraid so," Laney says in a solemn tone.

Grace looks at her with terrified blue eyes. "Is he gonna die?"

"I think so, sweetheart. But we should still pray for a miracle."

Letting out a sob, Grace falls onto her side and curls herself into a ball. Laney spoons her from behind, cooing encouraging words that everything will be okay when she's far from sure it will.

Grace's sobs eventually subside, and they drift off to sleep. When Laney's alarm goes off at six thirty on Friday morning, she reaches across her daughter to the nightstand, hitting the snooze button on her phone.

A small voice beside her says, "Please tell me it was a bad dream, that Granddaddy isn't dying."

Laney snuggles closer to her daughter, sniffing her strawberry shampoo. "I'm sorry, sweetheart. It wasn't a dream."

"Can I stay home from school today?"

Laney props herself on one elbow in order to see her daughter's face. "You don't want to miss your big game in Charlottesville this afternoon."

"Who cares about the game?" Grace says sniffling.

"Your teammates and coaches. You're the star player. They're counting on you to lead them to victory." Laney rolls out of bed and comes around to Grace's side. She pulls back the covers. "I know you're upset about Granddaddy, but I promise you'll feel better once you're at school with your friends."

Grace pushes herself to a sitting position. "Can I tell Ella?"

"Let's keep this between us for now. I'll make sure your father talks to her over the weekend."

"Okay." Grace gets to her feet and moves toward the door. "At least I understand now why Dad is so upset."

Laney holds her tongue. Hugh should be ashamed of himself. He's an adult. There's no good reason for him to behave like a lunatic.

———

Hugh's bedroom door is still closed when Laney leaves for work. She spends the morning creating bouquets and displaying them in her new iron rack on the sidewalk in front of the shop. Attracted by the display, customers leaving Delilah's Delights stop in to purchase a bouquet.

Laney chats them up as she processes their credit card charges. Many are hosting dinner parties tonight, while some simply want to brighten their kitchens. All are thrilled to finally have a local source for fresh flowers. They take her business card and promise to call with flower orders for special occasions soon.

By lunchtime, all the bouquets have been sold, and she puts together more. By three o'clock, every stem in her cooler is gone.

A delivery van from Flower Fanatics arrives around five o'clock with her flowers for this weekend's wedding, and she spends an hour getting organized for tomorrow morning's work.

Laney has nowhere she needs to be until eight o'clock when she picks the girls up from school. She's avoiding home, where she might run into Hugh. With time to kill, she goes upstairs to the small apartment. She opens all the windows in the living room to clear out the stuffy air. Sitting down on the sofa, she rests her head against the cushion and closes her eyes. She replays her conversation with Grace last night. Her girls are terrified. The three of them can't continue living in that house with their deranged father and husband. While it's not ideal, they can live in this apartment until they find something more suitable.

Hearing the crunch of gravel in the back alleyway, Laney gets up and walks to the window, surprised to see Bruce climbing out of his truck. She calls out to him, "Hey, there. What're you doing here?"

He holds up a bottle of champagne. "We're celebrating. Can I come up?"

"Sure. Use the door on the left. It should be unlocked."

Seconds later, footfalls on the steps precede Bruce's appearance in the doorway.

"What're we celebrating?" she asks, taking the champagne from him.

"Your new business. We can't let the occasion go unrecognized. And since you refuse to have an official grand opening, I had to take matters into my own hands." He removes a portable speaker from his back pocket. "I even brought tunes."

"Cool!" While he connects his phone to the speaker, Laney searches the kitchen for glasses. On the top shelf of a cabinet, she locates two dusty stemless champagne flutes. She rinses the glasses, and Bruce pops the cork.

"To Laney's Bouquets," he says, touching his glass to hers.

Laney giggles. "Thank you! Things are going well. I sold two batches of bouquets today. If I'd had more flowers, I could've sold more."

They drag chairs near the front windows where the cool autumn air is drifting in. Like a married couple, they take turns sharing news of what happened during the day. They've gotten to know each other well during their late-night phone calls. She's at ease with him in a way she never was with Hugh, but she warns herself to be careful. She has already fallen hard for this man. Her life is too complicated to act on those feelings.

When he moves to pour more champagne, she covers her glass with her hand. "I can't. I have to pick the girls up at school soon."

When an old Barbra Streisand song plays from the speaker, Bruce pulls Laney to her feet and into his arms. They dance in front of the window, gazing into each other's eyes. Their bodies fit perfectly together, and when he kisses her, she doesn't stop him. Their chemistry is powerful. This is where she's meant to be. But not like this. Not as secret lovers.

She pushes him away. "I can't do this, Bruce. Not while I'm still living with Hugh."

Bruce runs a hand through his auburn hair. "I'm so sorry, Laney. I didn't mean for that to happen. I can't control myself where you're concerned."

"I need you in my life. But friendship is all I have to offer for now. Maybe for a long time to come. If and when I finally get up the nerve to leave Hugh, I can't just jump into a relationship with you. I need to be alone to sort myself out."

Frustration crosses his handsome features. "You've been sleeping in your guest room for over a year. Isn't that the same as being alone?"

Laney considers this. "I guess so. But I have to think of my girls. They're going to need time to adjust."

He takes her hands in his. "I'm willing to wait as long as it takes, Laney. I'm crazy about you. You're my person, and I'm afraid of losing you. You need to leave Hugh. I'm terrified something bad will happen to you in that house."

"I'm getting close, Bruce. I just need a little more time." Laney takes their glasses to the kitchen, washing them out with soapy water and placing them on a paper towel to dry.

When she returns to the living room, he's standing at the window, staring out. "I hate to bust up this party, Bruce, but I need to leave to pick up the girls."

"Of course. Are you okay to drive?"

She smiles at him. "I'm fine. I only had the one glass."

They leave the apartment together, and Bruce walks her to her car. "I'm here for you, Laney. Call me anytime, night or day."

"I will. Maybe I'll see you tomorrow at the vineyard." She kisses his cheek, gets in her car, and drives off toward the school.

She arrives as the bus is pulling up. The team lost their game, and the girls say little on the way home. When she unlocks the door, Ella and Grace dart up the stairs, and Laney starts up after them.

Hugh's voice booms down the hall, stopping her in her tracks. "Laney! Get in here."

She freezes as she considers her options. She could ignore him and continue up the stairs. But she hasn't eaten since breakfast, and she's starving. He's in the room with the food, and she refuses to be a prisoner in her own home. She retraces her steps down the stairs.

Hugh, with feet apart and arms folded over chest, is waiting for her at the end of the hallway. "Where have you been?"

"At the shop, getting ready for the wedding tomorrow," she says, brushing past him.

He follows on her heels into the kitchen. "Are you having an affair?"

"I am. A love affair with my flowers." She opens the refrigerator and removes a plastic container of cold pasta salad.

He spins her around. "I'm not kidding, Laney. Don't you dare make a fool of me."

She keeps a straight face despite her racing mind. There was no one else in the apartment. He couldn't possibly know about Bruce. This is his obsession du jour. "I'm not having an affair, Hugh."

He narrows his deep blue eyes. "Swear to me."

She places her right hand over her heart. "I swear. I'm not having an affair," she says with a clean conscience. An innocent kiss doesn't constitute an affair.

Hugh runs a finger down her cheek. "Let's start over, babe. I'll give you whatever you want. Nicer car. Bigger house. I'm hoping we can move into Dad's house after he's gone."

Laney has often dreamed of being mistress of Love-Struck

Vineyard. The mansion is fabulous, but the price of having to stay married to Hugh is too great.

"Our problems are too deep-seated to work through on our own. We need marriage counseling." Laney says, shoveling pasta salad into her mouth.

"Rekindling our sex life would be a good start."

Laney levels her gaze on him. "Sex was never an issue. Your complete disregard for what's important to me is the problem."

"What could be more important than our family and our home?" he says, close enough for her to smell his rank whiskey breath.

"Nothing is more important than my girls, but my business is a close second." She returns the container to the refrigerator and slams the door shut.

"I don't understand. Why do you need to work when I've given you everything you've ever wanted?"

"It's not about material goods, Hugh. I need to be productive. I'm an artist. I need to create."

He snorts. "You call stuffing flowers in a vase art?"

"There you go again with your condescending attitude." Laney fills a tumbler with ice and water. "Your late-night drunken tirades have to stop. You're scaring the girls." She starts out of the room and turns back around. "By the way, Grace already knows about your father's medical condition. But you need to tell Ella tomorrow."

Laney bolts up the stairs, expecting him to follow, but is relieved when he doesn't. Sitting on the edge of her bed, she inhales and exhales deeply until her breath steadies. Hugh will never understand her, never accept her desire to make something of herself. She's fighting for her sanity, fighting for her future. She's no longer uncertain, no longer afraid. She needs to stop dragging out this unhealthy situation and start divorce proceedings. But she must be smart about it. She needs a plan.

CHAPTER 20
DANIEL

Late afternoon on Sunday, Daniel returns home from spending the weekend in Ruthie's bed to find Hugh dozing by the pool. When Daniel clears his throat, Hugh cracks an eyelid. "Finally. I've been waiting for you for hours."

"Looks to me like you were enjoying a little shut-eye while you were waiting." He touches his son's pink forearm. "Although you're going to need some aloe tonight after your shower."

Hugh glares at him. "Where have you been?"

Daniel lowers himself to the lounge chair beside his son. "Not that it's any of your business, but I have a lady friend. I've been with her all day."

Hugh looks at Daniel over the top of his aviator sunglass frames. "Oh really. Who?"

"Ruthie Poole. We've been seeing each other for years." After keeping Ruthie a secret for so long, it feels good to finally tell someone.

"Are you kidding me?" Hugh jerks the chair's back to a sitting position. "Why are you slumming with that blonde dingbat when you could have anyone you want?"

Heat pulses through Daniel's body. He's as angry at himself as he is with his son. He used to think the same thing about Ruthie.

How mistaken he's been about her. About so many things. If only he could turn back time. "Actually, Ruthie is too good for me. I'm grateful to have her in my life."

Hugh lets out a loud humph. "You're not planning to marry her, are you? I see no reason to complicate your estate planning at this stage in the game."

Daniel clenches his teeth. "By *stage in the game*, do you mean the last months of my life?"

"No sense in putting lipstick on a pig," Hugh says and looks away.

"Why are you here, Hugh? Did you need to see me about something?"

"I wanted to spend some time with you, Dad. I thought maybe we could hit some golf balls, but it's too late in the day for that now."

"We could play tennis and have dinner after." Already on his feet, Daniel says, "Come on, son. I could use the exercise."

Hugh trips along beside him as he hurries up the bluestone steps to the house. "Seriously, Dad. I haven't played tennis in years. I don't even own any tennis clothes."

"It's like riding a bike. You'll pick it back up. And I have some tennis whites you can borrow."

———

Hugh is no match for Daniel on the tennis court. He's in poor physical shape, and within minutes, Hugh's face is beet red, he's sweating like a pig, and he struggles to catch his breath. Daniel beats him six games to love in the first set. When he suggests a second set, Hugh begs off.

"I can't take any more. You crushed me. Are you sure the doctor didn't mistake your diagnosis? You seem in excellent shape to me."

Daniel ignores his son's question, his lies weighing heavily on him.

After showering in the men's locker room, Hugh and Daniel stroll over to the main clubhouse, where they are seated at a table for two on the terrace overlooking the eighteenth hole.

The server arrives promptly. Without looking at the menu, Daniel orders a salmon salad and a glass of pinot noir, and Hugh asks for the ribeye steak and a double Maker's Mark on ice.

"You should consider healthier eating habits, son. The extra weight you're carrying hindered your ability on the court."

"I prefer the mental challenge of golf," Hugh says.

"Actually, tennis has been proven to be equally as mentally challenging as golf."

Their drinks arrive, and Daniel sips his wine. "Cut to the chase, Hugh. Why did you really come to see me? What is it we need to discuss?"

Hugh gulps down half his drink. "You mentioned you have certain things you'd like to accomplish before . . ."

Daniel raises an eyebrow. "My demise?"

"This isn't funny, Dad." Hugh says, draining the whiskey and slamming his glass down on the table. "I want to hear about your projects and offer my assistance."

"Well, let's see." Daniel sits back and crosses his legs. "I'm enlarging the barrel building to encompass both private and public tasting rooms as well as more substantial and updated bottling equipment. I'll convert the cafe into an upscale bistro and expand the terrace seating area to include a large stone fireplace and fire pits. Once construction is finished next spring, in addition to serving lunch, we'll also be open for dinner. Of course, I won't be here to see the completion of these projects."

Hugh's eyes meet Daniel's. "You never know. Maybe you will be. I have some thought about an architect if you haven't already chosen one."

"I'm way ahead of you. I've been working with an architect for a while, and the plans are almost complete. I'm getting bids now. As soon as I decide which contractor to use, I'll share the plans with you and your siblings."

"About them . . . I was wondering how you intend to divvy up your shares in the company. Since I'm the oldest, I should be in control."

Daniel uncrosses his legs and sits up straight. "So that's what this is all about? I'll remind you that things didn't go so well the last time you were in charge."

"Whatever," Hugh says, and signals the server for another drink.

"You should go easy on the booze, son. Drunkenness doesn't become you."

"Maybe if you weren't so difficult to reason with, I wouldn't have to drink so much," Hugh snaps.

"I'm not being unreasonable. I'm being practical. Being the oldest doesn't automatically place you in a position of authority."

Hugh sits back in his chair with arms over chest. "If not me, then who?"

"Charles is out of the question. He can't tie his shoelaces without you watching him. Ideally, I'd like to see Sheldon and Casey running the winery and vineyard together. Perhaps you could oversee the bistro." Daniel presses his lips thin to suppress a smile. He's intentionally goading his son. Hugh can't wait for Daniel to die, and Daniel can't wait to see his son's face when Hugh finds out he's been magically cured.

"Seriously, Dad? When's the last time you saw Sheldon at the vineyard?"

Daniel doesn't answer, because he can't remember.

"That's what I thought. Sheldon hasn't come to work since his wedding. He's partnered up with Ollie. He's collaborating with our primary competition. You should demand his resignation."

"On the contrary. If Sheldon merged Love-Struck with Foxtail Farm, we'd have the largest vineyard in Virginia. I don't need to tell you what that would mean for us."

"That's a pipe dream. Ollie will never allow it."

"You never know." Daniel makes a mental note to discuss the

idea with Sheldon while Sheldon is sympathetic about his condition.

Hugh's drink arrives, and he makes a big show of gulping it all down at once. "As for Casey, I don't get your obsession with her. Until a few months ago, you had no clue she was alive."

"And I find that refreshing. She doesn't carry our family's baggage."

"Look, Dad." Hugh sets down his glass. "I realize I screwed up when I was in charge before. I was obsessed with buying Foxtail Farm and turning it into a luxury resort." He raises his pointer finger. "I still say it's a brilliant idea. But I understand now that it's not the right vision for Love-Struck's future. Can't you give me another chance to prove myself?"

Daniel's guilt gets the best of him, and he puts Hugh out of his misery. "Here's how this will go, son. I will allocate my shares, so the four of you—Sheldon, Casey, Charles, and you—have equal voting rights. Since you bought Ada out, you already have more shares than the others, which means you'll get less from me."

A flush creeps up Hugh's neck to his face. "How will we decide who's in charge?"

"That's up to the four of you. I'll be gone."

"What about The Nest? Who gets to live in your house?"

"The house and surrounding gardens belong to the vineyard. Whoever lives there will either pay rent or purchase the house outright at fair market value." Daniel moves to the edge of his seat. "I'm finding this discussion distasteful. I think I'll take my dinner home." He summons the server and asks for her to prepare his order to go.

Hugh hangs his head. "Don't go, Dad. I'm sorry if I upset you. I truly just want to help you accomplish your objectives."

"Really?" Daniel rises from his chair and leans over with both hands on the table. "Because you sound like the same what's-in-it-for-me Hugh you've been since you were a child. You've always been more than willing to throw your siblings under the bus to get what you want. I won't allow you to run Love-Struck until you learn to be a team player."

Hugh's eyes are dark with anger as he rises out of his chair to face him. "You're such a hypocrite. When have you ever been a team player? All our lives, you've insisted on having complete control over us. You're the king, and we're the peasants. You've pitted us against each other. It's like a sport to you, like pit bulls in a dogfight. You wouldn't know a team player if one smacked you in the ass."

"You are way out of line, son." Daniel wags his finger at him. "Keep this up, and I'll leave you out of my will entirely."

"There you go again, throwing your weight around. I'll get control of the vineyard if it's the last thing I do."

"I wouldn't count on it." Daniel snatches his take-out order from the approaching server and strides angrily across the terrace, ignoring the open stares from other diners.

He calms down enough on the drive home to realize Hugh is right about one thing. Daniel is not a team player, anymore than any of his children are team players. It'll never work for them to have equal control. Their bickering will have a negative impact on the vineyard. He'll do exactly what Hugh accused him of. He'll come up with a plan to pit his children against one another.

CHAPTER 21
LANEY

Laney waits until Hugh leaves for work on Monday morning before placing a call to Candice Wright, Ella's friend's mom, who is a divorce attorney. If necessary, she'll take out a bank loan to pay her fees.

The receptionist says, "I realize it's last minute, but our nine o'clock just canceled. If you can't make that, Mrs. Wright's next appointment is not until next week."

Laney glances at the clock on the stove. Eight thirty. Candice's office is only five minutes away. If she hurries, she can shower and still make it in time. "I'll take it. See you soon."

Thirty minutes later, the receptionist shows Laney to the divorce attorney's plush office. Candice is professional in a charcoal suit with black-framed glasses and her salt-and-pepper hair smoothed back in a low ponytail. If Candice is surprised to see Laney, she doesn't let it show. These office walls could undoubtedly weave a juicy tale of their small town's most troubled marriages.

Laney sits ramrod straight in the chair across the desk from Candice. "I guess I don't need to tell you why I'm here."

"Relax, Laney. You're in a safe place. You can trust me," Candice says with a kind smile that sets Laney at ease.

Exhaling slowly, Laney sits back in her chair and looks around the office. "I can't believe I'm actually here."

"I'm sure it took a lot of courage for you to come. And I'm eager to help you. Why don't you start at the beginning?" Candice says with a pen poised over a legal pad.

In detail, Laney tells her about her deteriorating marriage, including Hugh's erratic behavior of late.

"Has he physically hurt you?"

Hugh dragging her down the stairs seems like a small thing now. "Nothing major. I didn't call the police or anything."

"If it happens again, call them immediately, no matter how minor the infraction. Have you asked Hugh for a separation?"

"Many times. He threatened to kick me out of the house, get custody of the girls, and cut me off without a cent of alimony."

"He can't do any of that, anymore than you can. Virginia divorce laws are complicated. Unless you have evidence of adultery or physical abuse, you have no grounds to divorce him."

Laney's throat thickens. "I read that online. I was hoping you would know of a loophole."

"Unfortunately, I don't have better news for you. Your best option is to get him to agree to an uncontested divorce."

"That's easier said than done."

Candice leaves her chair and comes around to Laney's side of the desk. "Hang in there, Laney. In my experience, these things have a way of working themselves out."

Laney stands to go, and Candice walks her to the door. "We may not be close, but I consider you a friend. I'm here for you. You have my cell phone number. Do not hesitate to call, anytime day or night."

Laney leaves Candice's office with a heavy heart. When she arrives at the flower shop, the sight of her overturned metal shelving unit causes the damn to break, and she bursts into tears. Lowering herself to a nearby stool, she plants her elbows on the worktable, buries her face in her hands, and sobs until her well is dry.

Pulling herself together, she sets about cleaning up the mess. Fortunately, most of her containers are still in the back of her Suburban from the wedding on Saturday, and only two glass cubes were destroyed. She's sweeping up the broken glass when Bruce calls.

"How'd it go with the attorney?"

"As expected. Either I get Hugh to agree to the divorce or I'm stuck with him for the rest of my life."

Bruce sighs. "I don't understand it."

"Neither do I, but it's Virginia law."

"How are things at Laney's Bouquets today?" he asks with a failed attempt at sounding cheerful.

Laney eyes the shelving on the floor. "Fine, except my metal shelves toppled over. Either the floor is uneven, or the unit is top heavy."

"I can fix that with a pair of L brackets. I'm stuck at work until around four. On my way over, I will stop by the hardware store.

"That'd be great. Thanks so much, Bruce." She drops the phone onto the worktable with a thunk. Normally, the possibility of seeing him would excite her. But there is zero chance they'll ever be together unless she commits adultery. She considers the possibility for a split second before forcing it from her mind. Her daughters and her integrity are all she has left. She'll have to figure out a way to make the most of a difficult situation.

After unloading her car, Laney settles in at the table to finalize plans for future weddings. She's only been working a few minutes when there's a knock at the front door. She's surprised to see Ada standing beneath the awning."

"Congratulations on your new store! This is fabulous, Laney. I'm so happy for you."

Laney's lips part in a genuine smile. "Thank you. It's a dream come true."

"Is this a good time to talk about flowers for my wedding? If not, I can come back later."

"This is a great time. Come on in. I'm not officially open for business yet. I won't have regular hours until I can afford to hire an assistant." Laney locks the door behind Ada and shows her to the back room. They sit down together at the table, and Laney flips her legal pad to a clean page. "Do you know what style of flowers and color scheme you want?" Laney palms her forehead. "What am I thinking? You're Ada Love. I'm sure you know exactly what you want."

Ada smiles. "I have an idea, but I trust your impeccable taste, and I want your honest feedback."

"I appreciate your vote of confidence. As you're aware, this time of year offers many choices."

"I love the yellows and purples and oranges of autumn flowers. But Casey's dress is a soft sage color, and I think all white might be best."

Laney looks up from her legal pad. "Casey is in your wedding?"

"She's my only attendant, my maid of honor," Ada says.

Laney stares at her in disbelief. "But I thought you and Casey were arch enemies."

Ada dismisses Laney's comment with a flick of the wrist. "We've decided to put all that unpleasantness behind us. Tell me the truth. Do You think white flowers are boring?"

Laney returns to making notes. "Not if you use the right white flowers. There's nothing more elegant than white flowers with pretty greenery. You could incorporate your mama's five-prong Tiffany candelabra on the main table." She taps her pen on the table as her creative wheels spin. "Actually, if Daniel will let us use them, there are several handsome accents at The Nest, like those large antique blue-and-white porcelain vases in the center hallway."

Ada stabs a red lacquered fingernail at her. "I like the way you're thinking."

"If you get Daniel's permission, we can walk through the house to see what else we can find." Laney opens her computer, and they spend a few minutes looking at photographs on Pinterest, adding the ones they like best to a board designated for Ada's wedding.

"Now that I know what you want, I'll talk to my wholesaler and come up with a plan. I'll get a proposal to you in a few days."

"Perfect!" Ada jumps up. "I'm actually getting excited about the wedding."

"After all you've been through these past few months, you deserve some happiness," Laney says, following Ada through the swinging door into the showroom.

When she reaches the door, Ada turns to face her. "So do you, Laney. It's been a long time since I've seen you happy. My brother is not an easy man. I can't imagine what it must be like to be married to him. If you ever need to talk, I'm right across the street. Now that we're shop neighbors, we'll be seeing more of each other."

Laney's throat swells, and she asks in a tight voice, "When's your grand opening?"

"This Wednesday, from three to six. I hope you'll stop by."

"I can hardly wait," Laney says, making a mental note to take Ada a celebratory arrangement for her event.

After Ada is gone, Laney returns to her notes. For the next two hours, she makes sketches of arrangements and writes up proposals. When Bruce doesn't show up at five o'clock, she gets worried. She texts him, but he doesn't respond. She's about to give up on him when she hears his truck in the back alley around five thirty. Seconds later, he comes through the back door with his toolbox and a little brown bag from the hardware store.

"I'm sorry I'm late," he says, setting his toolbox on the ground beside the overturned shelving unit. "Country Craftsman is not your normal hardware store. They sell some seriously cool stuff. I got hung up in the outdoor grill section. I'm ready to buy a house just to have a place for my grill."

Laney giggles. "You missed your calling. Instead of being a winemaker, you should own a hardware store."

"Ironic that you say that. Country Craftsman is for sale. If I didn't love what I do, I'd consider buying it."

Bruce rights the shelf and sets about fastening it to the wall. Once the wall is secure, he helps Laney load it up with supplies and containers.

He puts away his tools and closes his toolbox. "You wanna tell me more about your meeting with the divorce attorney?"

"As I told you earlier, it's not good news," Laney says, and gives him a brief recount of her meeting with Candice. "Short of moving to a state with more lenient divorce laws, I'm stuck with Hugh for the time being."

Bruce squeezes her arm. "I'm sorry, Laney. But don't give up. We'll find another way."

"I can't ask you to wait for me, Bruce. It could be years. You'd be wasting your life," she says as tears fill her eyes.

Bruce pulls her into his arms. "I'm not leaving you, Laney. I'll be fine. It's you I'm worried about."

On the threshold of a breakdown, she wrenches free of him. "I have to go, Bruce."

He pinches his brow. "Are you sure? I hate to leave you when you're so upset."

"I need to be alone right now," Laney says, gathering her things.

"I understand." He grabs his toolbox, and they exit the building together. He calls out to her as she gets in her Suburban. "Call me later if you can."

Laney drives at a snail's pace on her way home, taking deep breaths to calm her frazzled nerves. She's planned nothing for dinner, and she's in no mood to go to the market. She'll wait until the girls get home, and they'll order Mexican takeout. Even the girls are growing tired of pizza.

She's pulled herself together by the time she arrives home. Hugh is seated at the kitchen counter with a manila file and the ever-present bottle of whiskey in front of him.

"Where have you been?" he asks in an accusatory tone.

"At work, writing up proposals," she says, retrieving an open bottle of pinot grigio from the refrigerator.

"You swore to me you aren't having an affair."

She freezes, the wine bottle poised near a glass. "I'm not."

He opens the file and slides a photograph across the counter. "Then explain this."

She glances down, then does a double take at the image of herself and Bruce kissing in the apartment's window above the shop. The earth falls away beneath her, but she maintains her composure. "I'm not having an affair. It was one kiss. It shouldn't have happened." She lifts the photograph and studies it more closely. Whoever took it was standing across the street near Ada's wine shop. They must have used a superzoom lens to get such a clear image. "How'd you get this anyway?"

"I hired a private investigator." He slides another photograph across the counter. "He took this one earlier today. After your meeting with a divorce attorney."

Laney stares at the picture of herself emerging from Candice's office building. "Candice isn't my attorney. She and I are planning an end-of-season party for the hockey team."

He bangs his fist on the counter. "Stop lying." He gets up and comes around to her side of the counter. "I consulted my own divorce attorney. You don't have any evidence against me to apply for a contested divorce. But I do," he says, snatching the incriminating photograph from her hands.

"Good! Then divorce me! Better yet, let's agree to an uncontested divorce."

He sneers at her. "And give you half of everything I own? No thanks. I've made it clear I don't want a divorce. You have two choices. You can return to my bed, and we can work on rebuilding our marriage. Or I will plaster this photograph all over social media."

"So plaster it! See if I care," she says, taking a large gulp of wine.

"You'll care when your boyfriend loses his job at Love-Struck.

You know how Dad is about preserving the family's image at all costs. As much as Dad loves Bruce, he'll give him the axe in a second to avoid a scandal. Are you sure you want to ruin Bruce's career?"

Laney's knees go weak, and she grabs hold of the counter for support. "No," she says in a meek voice. Hugh has outplayed her for now. But she'll figure out a way to get out of this marriage if it's the last thing she does.

CHAPTER 22
ADA

Ada is delighted to see Laney in the small crowd gathered at the front of Primo Vino for the ribbon cutting ceremony. Something about her sister-in-law seemed off during their visit on Monday. Her eyes were sad, and despite her sunny demeanor, she appeared troubled, as though something were on her mind. But today, Laney's smile is bright from behind an elaborate arrangement of orchid plants.

Enzo finger-whistles to get everyone's attention. "I'd like to thank you all for coming today, to help us celebrate our grand opening. Ada and I are grateful for your support, and we look forward to sharing many glasses of wine with you in the years to come." He brandishes a pair of scissors. "And now, without further ado." He snips the ribbon and cheers erupt from the group.

Laney, with her orchids, moves toward Ada. "Congratulations on your new business."

"These are gorgeous, Laney. You really have a natural flair for floral design." Ada walks the arrangement over to the checkout counter near the front window. "I'll leave them here where everyone can see."

Laney produces a small stack of business cards. "Would you

mind if I left these on the counter beside the orchids? If your clients are purchasing wine for a dinner party, they might be interested in buying flowers as well."

"Good point. I'll give you plugs if you do the same for me." Ada takes a few of her own business cards off the stack beside the point-of-sale terminal.

Laney pockets the cards. "Absolutely. Isn't this fun?" She shivers as though with excitement. "First a florist, and now a wine shop. Our little town is coming up in the world."

Ada gives her a half hug. "Who knew you and I would be such trendsetters?" She gestures at the tastings taking place at the individual stations in the center of the shop. "Go! Drink some wine. Representatives from several local vineyards are pouring their finest."

Laney's blue eyes survey the crowd. "Is anyone here from Love-Struck?"

Ada leans in close and whispers, "We pride ourselves on being selective. Love-Struck's wines aren't up to par yet."

"They'll get there. Bruce is working his magic," Laney says, her features softening.

Her sister-in-law's dreamy expression confuses Ada. Is something going on between Laney and Bruce?

"Anyway, I can't stay. I have a ton of work to do. Good luck with everything today. If you need anything, I'm right across the street," Laney says, kissing her cheek in parting.

Ada smiles at her. "Thanks again for the orchids."

Laney has no sooner exited the building when Daniel arrives. He sips all the wines and purchases several mixed cases. His wine cellar at The Nest is already overflowing. He needs more wine like Ada needs more designer shoes. But he's being supportive, and she appreciates the gesture.

"Casey tells me the wedding plans are coming along," Daniel says as he swipes his card through the card reader. "It thrilled me to hear you'd asked her to be your maid of honor. I can leave this earth in peace, knowing you finally got the sister you always wanted."

Ada smiles, despite never having expressed a desire for a sister. She loved having three older brothers dote on her.

She processes the charge and hands Daniel a receipt. "We'll have the wine sent out to the house tomorrow."

For the rest of the afternoon, a steady stream of locals passes through the shop. Some taste, others buy multiple bottles of wine, and a few simply browse, checking out the store.

Ollie and Sheldon enter the shop around five o'clock. Sheldon makes a beeline for the wine tasting while Ollie moseys over to Ada at the checkout counter.

"You look amazing," Ada says. "Look at your baby bump. Do you mind if I touch it?"

Ollie laughs. "Be my guest. I might as well get used to everyone pawing my belly."

As she palms Ollie's belly, Ada has a sudden yearn for a baby of her own.

"I hope you don't mind us stealing Melvin from you," Ada says about their part-time sales associate.

Ollie laughs. "You're doing me a favor, honestly. Melvin is the most vibrant seventy-year-old I've ever met. He has ten times the energy I do. I can't find enough projects to keep him busy. He'll make an excellent sales associate. No one knows Virginia wines like Melvin."

"And he's so charming. Everyone loves him," Ada says, watching Melvin engage with a young couple.

Ollie clears her throat and lowers her voice. "Enzo may need to speak with Melvin about his attire, though. Better yet, he should take him shopping. Melvin started over here earlier, dressed in overalls. I insisted he change. I think what he's wearing is the best outfit he owns."

Ada eyes Melvin's faded blue jeans and plaid flannel shirt. "I'm fine with his attire. But I imagine our clients expect our sales-people to be a little more current."

Ollie stands on her tiptoes to see over the crowd. "I'd better go find my husband. He's liable to drink all your wine."

Ada laughs. "That's not possible. We have so much wine we can barely fit in the storage room."

When Ollie wanders off, Ada moves to the display case to inspect her cheeses. She's proud of her artful display and careful selection of goat and cow cheeses. While she's disappointed Sally West couldn't make it to the opening, she's excited to see the cheeses from Shady Creek Creamery are selling well.

She's replenishing the stock when a familiar voice says, "Nice place."

Ada cranes her neck to see Stuart looming over her. "Thanks," she says, and returns her attention to her task.

"You made the right choice in disclaiming your inheritance. You have plenty to occupy your time here." He chuckles, a sound that's more malicious than amused. "I admit it surprised me when you gave in to my threats so easily. Daniel gave me the impression you were a fighter."

Ada spins around to face him. "Since when have you been discussing me with Daniel?"

"He invited me to lunch a few weeks back. He asked me to help him get you away from my father." Stuart inspects his mani-cured fingernails. "I would have come after you anyway, when I discovered Dad had changed his will. You, as his bastard child, have no right to any of Dad's properties or investments."

Ada shifts her gaze slightly right to Bud, who is standing behind Stuart, eavesdropping on their conversation. He presses his finger to his lips, warning Ada not to acknowledge his presence.

Ada returns her attention to Stuart. "Let me get this straight. You're saying Daniel intentionally sabotaged my relationship with Bud?"

"Wow. You're a quick learner, Ada." A smirk appears on his lips. "Of course, Daniel lost interest in my efforts when his terminal cancer diagnosis sent you running back to him like a dutiful daughter. Which tells me you were never interested in having a relationship with Bud. You only wanted to get your hands on his equestrian farm."

Raging fury bowls Ada over, taking her breath. "You're out of your damn mind." Her eyes dart back and forth between Bud and Stuart before landing on Bud. "All I ever wanted from you was to know my biological father, no strings attached."

Stuart's head snaps back as he realizes his father is standing beside him. "Dad! I didn't see you there."

Ada shoves her way past Stuart, grabs her purse from under the checkout counter, and leaves the shop. Her temper boils as she speeds through town and down the mountain road to Love-Struck. She's furious at Daniel, but she's even more livid at herself for falling into his trap.

The absence of Daniel's car in the driveway doesn't deter her. She parks haphazardly and bursts through the front door. Hearing voices at the back of the house, she marches down the center hall to the kitchen. Marabella, her purse slung over one shoulder as though preparing to leave for the day, is chatting with a young man Ada has never seen before.

Marabella stops talking when she sees Ada in the doorway. "Well, look who's here. I haven't seen you in ages." She drops her purse on the counter and extends her arms. "Come here and give Marabella a hug."

Her emotions near the surface as Ada walks into the cook's outstretched arms.

"Lord, child. You're shaking all over." She holds her at arm's length. "What's wrong?"

"I'm upset," Ada says, choking back a sob.

"I can see that." Marabella walks Ada over to the breakfast counter. "Sit down and let me fix you some sweet tea."

"I'm fine. And it's time for you to go home anyway." Ada tries to stand up, but Marabella pushes her back down.

"We can spare a few minutes. Can't we, Claude?" Marabella doesn't give the young man a chance to respond. "This is my nephew, by the way. He's taking me to pick up my car from the mechanic."

Ada nods her greeting, and he flashes her a bright smile.

Marabella fills two glasses with ice and tea, giving one to Ada and the other to Claude. She sits down next to Ada while Claude leans against the wall near the door. "Talk to me, baby. Tell Marabella what happened."

Ada explains how Daniel colluded with Stuart to turn Ada against Bud. "Turns out Daniel didn't need Stuart after all. His cancer diagnosis got him what he wanted. Me, a heartsick little girl crying over her terminally ill father."

"Wait a minute," Claude says, pushing off the wall. "Since when is Daniel's cancer terminal?"

Ada narrows her eyes suspiciously at him. "What do you know about his illness?"

"Claude is a certified nursing assistant," Marabella explains. "He attended to Daniel when he had his surgery in Charlottesville."

Claude moves closer to them. "And I was in the room when the surgeon read Mr. Love's pathology report. The doctor got all the cancer during the operation. No chemo or radiation was recommended as follow-up treatment."

Ada shoots out of her chair and gets in Claude's face. "You mean to tell me Daniel has been faking like he's dying?"

Claude takes a step back. "Maybe. But don't take my word for it. You should ask Mr. Love."

As if on cue, Daniel appears in the doorway. "Ask me what?"

Ada crosses the kitchen in three strides. "Are you or aren't you terminally ill with pancreatic cancer?"

The color drains from Daniel's face. "I . . . um," he begins, with shoulders slumping. "I exaggerated my condition, hoping to elicit sympathy from you. I had colon cancer. But the doctor was successful in removing it during surgery."

She pins him against the wall with a death stare. "You've done some terrible things, Daniel Love. But this takes the cake. Stupid me. I took the bait—hook, line, and sinker. But never again. As of this moment, you're out of my life for good."

Daniel appears stricken. "You don't mean that."

"Like hell I don't," Ada says and storms out of the kitchen.

Daniel calls after her, "Ada! Wait! Come back."

Ada increases her pace, hurrying down the hall and out of the house to the safety of her car. She doesn't look in the rearview mirror as she drives away from her childhood home, potentially for the last time. On the passenger seat beside her, she roots around in her purse for her phone. She thumbs through her favorites list, deciding who she should call first before clicking on Casey's number.

"You're not gonna believe this," she says when Casey answers on the second ring. "Daniel has been faking his illness. He had colon cancer, but the doctor removed all the cancer during his surgery."

Casey pauses a beat. "You mean he's not dying?"

"Not from cancer. Although I may very well strangle him with my bare hands."

"That's insane. Who would do such a thing?" Casey asks in an incredulous tone.

Ada tightens her grip on the steering wheel. "Only a sick bastard like Daniel."

"Where are you?"

"On the way back to Primo Vino." Ada reaches Magnolia Avenue and makes a left-hand turn. "I'm almost there, actually."

"I'm at my condo. I'll meet you downstairs in a minute. Do you want me to call Sheldon?"

Ada pauses while she considers how to handle the situation. "Yes, but I want to be the one to tell him. Ask Sheldon to text the others and have them come to the wine shop right away. We need to discuss how to handle the situation. Word will soon get out, and we must figure out how to do damage control."

CHAPTER 23
LANEY

For two days, Laney avoids Bruce. But when he appears at the shop's back door around five o'clock Wednesday afternoon, she can no longer postpone the inevitable. For the sake of Bruce's career, she must end their friendship. While Hugh has yet to post the photograph of Laney and Bruce kissing on social media, he's using it as leverage. He wants Laney to give their marriage another chance, and she's playing along with him for now.

Laney steps out into the alley. "You can't be here, Bruce. I'm still being followed."

"How can you tell?" he asks with concern written on his handsome features.

"Because I've been hyperalert. A black sedan has been following me, and I sense someone watching me." Laney stares down at the ground, kicking at pebbles. "Whatever this thing is between us must end. I owe it to my girls to give my marriage another chance." As the lie leaves her lips, a sharp pain penetrates her chest.

"So, you're going back to him, just like that?" Bruce snaps his fingers. "Without even putting up a fight?"

She glares at Bruce. "Technically, I never left him. Besides, with no grounds for divorce, what choice do I have?"

"Don't do this, Laney. You're wasting your life and your happiness on a man who doesn't appreciate you. Run away with me. There are states that allow for quick divorces."

"But none that will grant me custody of my daughters. I'm sorry, Bruce. If you ask me to choose between you and my girls, they win."

Bruce leans against the side of the building. "Of course they do. That was insensitive of me. I'm in love with you, Laney. I can't let you go."

Her heart skips a beat at the sound of the words she's longed to hear. But they are meaningless now. "If you really care about me, you'll leave me alone. You have to trust that this is for the best." She goes inside the flower shop and locks the door.

Propping herself against the door, she holds back her emotions until she hears Bruce's truck leave. She sits down at the table and buries her face in her hands. Laney is so tired of crying, so tired of constantly obsessing about her marital problems. With Bruce out of the way, she can put her plan into motion.

She will cook Hugh a nice dinner tonight, make certain he drinks too much, and antagonize him into attacking her. She's willing to suffer any amount of pain if it means getting rid of him.

The handgun she stole from his gun safe is heavy in her handbag as she locks up for the day. She knows how to shoot the gun, and she'll use it if necessary to protect herself and her girls.

After stopping by the grocery store, Laney is on her way home about six fifteen when Hugh calls. She's tempted to let it go to voice mail, but he calls so rarely these days it might be important. She answers with a tentative *hello*.

"Laney! I'm glad I reached you. I just got a text from Sheldon about a family emergency. We're meeting at Ada's wine shop. Get over there as soon as you can."

"What sort of family emergency?"

"He didn't say. Something to do with Dad."

"Don't drag me into your family drama, Hugh. You go ahead without me. I'll have dinner waiting when you get home."

"It's important we present a united front with my siblings. I'll see you in a few minutes." He ends the call before she can argue.

Curious about the family emergency, Laney makes a U-turn and heads back toward Magnolia Avenue.

When the small lot behind Primo Vino is full, Laney parks in front of her flower shop. She crosses the street, and as she approaches Primo Vino, she hears shouting coming from within. She slips in the door unnoticed and inches close to Charles's wife, Hazel.

"What happened?" she whispers. "Why is everyone so angry?"

Hazel cups her hand over her mouth. "Apparently Daniel was pretending to be dying."

Laney gasps. "That's the most twisted thing I've ever heard."

Hazel crosses her eyes. "Right?"

Laney tunes into what Ada is saying. "I'm done with Daniel Love. He's not my father. Handle this however you want. But leave me out of it."

When more arguing erupts, Charles takes Hazel by the arm and drags her out the front door. Laney makes her way over to Hugh's side. She can feel the heat emanating from his body. He's furious. Daniel's not dying, which means Hugh won't be inheriting the vineyard.

"Quiet!" Sheldon shouts over the angry roar. "Everyone, listen up! What Dad has done to us is unacceptable, and we can't let him get away with it. But we're too upset to make any major decisions tonight."

"What do we do when word of his betrayal leaks out?" Casey asks.

"We tell the truth," Sheldon says. "We shouldn't cover for him. He's dug his grave. He has to lie in it."

Hugh steps forward, speaking for the first time. "I disagree.

This will destroy our family's reputation and put the vineyard in jeopardy."

"Who else knows about this?" Sheldon asks Ada.

"Only Marabella and her nephew, Claude."

"I'll reach out to Marabella in the morning. We can trust her to be discreet. Let's all keep this to ourselves for now. Go home, and try to get some sleep." Sheldon takes his pregnant wife by the hand and leads her to the door.

"I'll see you at home," Laney says to Hugh and hurries out ahead of him. With Hugh so upset about his inheritance, Laney should easily be able to push him over the edge.

She speeds to the house and quickly unloads her groceries from the car. When Hugh arrives fifteen minutes later, she's sauteing breaded chicken breasts while guzzling white wine. She figures the beating will hurt less if she's drunk.

Retrieving a bottle of whiskey from the liquor cabinet, Hugh drops to a bar stool, pours a shot, gulps it down, and pours another. He rants on about his father's deception, growing louder and drunker and playing right into Laney's hand. She offers a sympathetic mm-hmm every few minutes while she assembles a chicken Parmesan casserole. She'll wait a few more minutes before she pokes the bear.

"How could he do this to me?" Hugh cries.

Laney slides the casserole into the oven. "You're not the only one affected by his actions. You have brothers and sisters. Think about Ada. He tricked her into having her wedding at Love-Struck."

Hugh jumps to his feet and comes around to her side of the counter. "Ada is no longer a part of this family. She's not his daughter."

"Maybe not in the technical sense, but Daniel clearly still thinks of her as his daughter. That's why he did all this. To get Ada back in his life. He's gone to extraordinary measures to host her dream wedding."

Hugh's jaw tightens. "So what?"

"Admit it, Hugh. That's why you're so angry. Because Daniel loves Ada more than you, and she's not even his daughter."

A vein at Hugh's temple pulses. "Shut up, Laney."

Laney squeezes her eyes shut, preparing herself for the first blow. When nothing happens, she cracks an eyelid to find him drinking whiskey directly from the bottle.

"You have no idea why I'm so angry." He thrusts the whiskey bottle at her and brown liquid splashes onto her blouse.

Laney blots at her blouse with a kitchen towel. "Then explain it to me," she says, even though she knows full well what's driving his fury.

"Dad's not dying. Which means I'm not getting my inheritance. Which means you don't get to live at The Nest."

Laney's jaw drops with feigned surprise. "I can't believe you just said that. Is money all you ever think about?"

"Pretty much." He palms her face. "Money and having sex with you."

Laney smacks his hand away. "I'm never having sex with you again, Hugh. Get that through your thick head."

"You'll feel differently when I'm the King Kahuna at Love-Struck. My siblings will distance themselves from Dad to punish him for his deception. When they do, I'll use the opportunity to ease my way into his good graces."

"You're delusional. Daniel will never pick you over them."

Hugh's face beams red and nostrils flare. "Why, you little bitch!"

She tenses her body as she braces for impact. "Go ahead, hit me."

He throws his head back and lets out a maniacal laugh that sends shivers down her spine. "So that's what this is all about? You want me to give you a black eye so you can go running to the police." Grabbing a fistful of her blouse, he pulls her face close to his. "You can antagonize me all you want, but I will never be so stupid as to leave a mark on you." He shoves her away and then pins her against the counter with his body. "You don't know who you're up against, Laney. I will beat you down, and I will eventually get my way. You'll come running back to me, begging for forgiveness."

She snatches a knife from the counter behind her. "Don't hold your breath," she says, brandishing the knife at his face.

"Don't do it, Laney. You cut me, you go to jail."

Laney hears her daughters' voices in the foyer. Turning her back on Hugh, she returns the knife to the butcher block. Hugh may have won this first battle, but she has every intention of winning the war.

CHAPTER 24
DANIEL

Daniel never stopped to consider what would happen if his family found him out. He made the fatal error of assuming Claude would never cross paths with any of his loved ones. He should've paid Claude for his silence when he had the chance. Even Marabella is angry at him. She left the house without saying goodbye, which she has never done in all her decades of working for him.

Ada will undoubtedly tell the others, his legitimate children, and they will understandably be hurt and angry. But they'll eventually calm down. Because Daniel is not only their father, he's their boss. Now might be a good time to remind them what's at stake if they turn against him.

Ada is a different matter, however. He worked so hard to get back in her good graces and now this. Her wedding plans are underway, which plays in his favor. She wouldn't dare cancel at this late date because of a little misunderstanding. Or would she?

Ruthie is the person he's most worried about. He needs to confess the truth before she hears it from someone else. Things are going so well between them. He has no intention of losing her again.

Daniel checks out the contents of his refrigerator before calling her. "I realize this is short notice, but can you come for dinner tonight? Marabella made her famous shrimp and feta casserole. I think you'll really like it."

"What gives, Daniel? In all the ten years we've been together, you've never once invited me to The Nest."

"There's a first time for everything." His voice grows softer and his tone more serious. "I have something important I need to talk to you about. It feels right to have the conversation here."

"In that case, what can I bring?"

"Nothing, unless you have some of your famous cheddar muffins handy," Daniel says removing a chilled bottle of sauvignon blanc from his wine cooler.

"I made a fresh batch this afternoon."

"Awesome. And bring a change of clothes for in the morning. We're having a sleepover."

Ending the call, he pours a glass of wine and takes it to his study. Sliding back a panel in his bookcase, he spins the dial on his wall safe and removes a black velvet ring box.

Seated at his desk, he opens the box and admires the engagement ring. The diamond isn't as flashy as the one he'd purchased for his wife, but the quality is exceptional. He bought this ring for Beverly Hobbs, Casey's mother, during their summer-long affair in Napa Valley. He loved Beverly enough to risk losing his family and his business. But when he proposed, she turned him down. She refused to tear his family apart.

Daniel removes the ring from the box and slips it in his pocket. It will look lovely on Ruthie's delicate finger. She'll never know he bought it for another woman.

So what if Ruthie's a little rough around the edges? Not only does she have a big heart, she's drop-dead gorgeous and smoking hot in bed. He'll transform her into a sophisticated woman with designer clothes and a more subdued hairstyle.

Daniel returns to the kitchen and places the casserole in the oven. He's icing a bottle of champagne when the front doorbell rings.

Ruthie, dressed in a slinky purple dress and sandals, thrusts a basket of muffins and her overnight bag at him. "Do I get a tour?"

"Of course." He takes the muffins to the kitchen, pours her a glass of wine, and spends the next thirty minutes showing her the house and grounds.

Down at the pool, she slides her foot out of her sandal and dips a toe in the water. "Ooh. It's so warm. You should've told me to bring my bathing suit."

"Why do we need bathing suits?" he asks, taking her in his arms.

Ruthie feigns horror. "Why you naughty man! Are you suggesting we skinny-dip?"

"That's exactly what I'm suggesting," he says, his mouth covering hers.

She playfully pushes him away. "Can we eat first? I'm starving."

"You bet." He takes her by the hand and leads her back to the kitchen.

Ruthie sets the table on the terrace while Daniel finishes preparing dinner. When they sit down together, Ruthie asks "What did you want to talk to me about? It must be pretty important for you to invite me here."

"I realize this will come as a surprise to you, as hard as I have pushed back against the idea of us getting married. But these past couple of weeks have been amazing, and I want to spend all my time with you." He removes the ring from his pocket and slides it on her finger.

Ruthie gasps. "It's gorgeous." When she removes her hand from his, the ring slips off her finger and clatters onto the table.

Daniel's face warms. "We'll have that fixed. I guessed at the size. Clearly, I was wrong."

Ruthie picks up the ring and studies it closely. "It's truly beautiful, Daniel. But I don't understand. Do we really need this complication in our lives? Where will we even live? Here or at my house?" She sets the ring down on the table. "I don't see the point of us getting married when you have so little time left."

"About that." Daniel intertwines his fingers. "I have a confession to make."

Ruthie falls back in her chair. "I knew there had to be a catch."

"I'm not dying, Ruthie. I had colon cancer, but I had an operation, and the oncologist surgeon got it all. My intentions were honorable, even though I stretched the truth a little.

She stares at him with mouth agape. "There's nothing honorable about lying, Daniel. You've done some shady stuff in the past, but I never thought you were capable of something so underhanded . . . so insensitive . . . You don't know how much I've cried over the prospect of losing you."

"I know this is bad, Ruthie. And I'm so incredibly sorry. When I came up with this plan, I didn't think about the hurt I would cause. I was desperate to get you back. I used the situation to elicit sympathy from you, so you'd give me another chance."

"And I fell right into your trap," she says, her face flushed with anger.

"I realize I screwed up. But I'm trying to make it up to you by marrying you."

"How generous of you." She picks up the engagement ring. "If you were serious about marrying me, you would've taken the time to find out my ring size. You didn't buy this ring for me. Whose ring is it, Daniel?"

"It belonged to one of my ancestor's," Daniel lies. "Passing down family heirloom jewelry is what families like mine do. You should feel privileged to wear it."

"It doesn't look like an antique." She throws the ring at him and jumps to her feet. "This is the last straw, Daniel. You won't get another chance with me." She spins on her heels and disappears inside the house.

When Daniel makes a move to go after her, dizziness overcomes him, and he falls back in his chair. This isn't like the bouts of vertigo he occasionally suffers. And it's not the first time it's happened either. He should probably see his doctor. But Jason would have heard the rumors about Daniel's imminent demise, and he would have received the pathologist report from the oncologist surgeon in Charlottesville declaring him cancer free. Daniel dreads having to explain why he lied.

Daniel hears Ruthie's car start in the driveway, followed by the screech of rubber against pavement as she speeds off. He remains at the table for a long while, contemplating the disaster he's made of his life. When he swipes at his eyes, he's surprised to find his face wet. When was the last time he cried? He's shocked to realize that it wasn't when his wife died. It was when Casey's mother ended their relationship.

Daniel clears the untouched plates from the table and takes the ring back to his study. Returning the ring to the box, he drops it into his top desk drawer. He'll give it to Casey. She should have it. After all, he'd bought it for her mother.

Pouring himself two fingers of brandy, he retires to his bedroom. The sight of Ruthie's overnight bag on his bed brings a lump to his throat. He unzips the bag and removes the lingerie—black, lacy, and sexy as hell. Ruthie has an impressive collection of teddies and bustiers and baby doll gowns. Never has he seen this set. She was saving it for a special occasion. They were supposed to get engaged tonight.

Daniel falls back against the pillows and sobs unrestrainedly. So this is what young women mean by ugly crying. The guilt and heartache are acute. If only God would make the pain go away, he will promise to be a better man.

CHAPTER 25
ADA

Yesterday's events come crashing back the minute Ada opens her eyes on Thursday morning. "Ugh," she whispers, sliding deeper under the plush duvet.

Next to her, Enzo lets out a grunt. "Right? Gives new meaning to rude awakening."

Rolling onto her side, she hooks an arm around his waist. "How long have you been awake?"

"For hours. Worrying about our wedding. What're we gonna do?"

"Good question. I'd suggest we cancel it, except I have my heart set on marrying you, on us being husband and wife when we move into our new home."

He turns to face her. "So we'll keep the date and change the venue."

"And scratch the guest list except for family and a few friends."

"Minus Daniel love."

"For sure." Ada pushes herself up against the headboard. "Question is, Where will we find an available venue at this late date?"

"We'll call around. I'm sure we can find something some-where," he says, but his tone lacks confidence.

Ada grabs her phone off the nightstand and scrolls through her texts. "Sheldon invited us to Foxtail Farm for breakfast at eight thirty. We should probably go, although I'm not sure I'm up for another family meeting."

Enzo smacks his forehead with the palm of his hand. "With everything that happened yesterday, I forgot to tell you I asked Sheldon to be my best man."

Ada smiles at him. "That makes me so happy, Enzo. I'm thrilled you and Sheldon are becoming friends." She throws her legs over the side of the bed and moves toward the bathroom. "We need to get a move on if we're going to make it to Foxtail by eight thirty."

Enzo flings back the covers and runs after her. "Since time is of the essence, we should definitely shower together."

———

Enzo and Ada are ten minutes late for breakfast, but Ollie is still setting the table on the screened porch when they arrive.

"Morning," she says, placing red checkered linen napkins at each place. "We're running a few minutes behind. Sheldon is mixing up a pitcher of mimosas in the kitchen, if you're interested."

Ada's hand shoots up. "I'm interested. I need booze to numb the pain of what Daniel has done to us."

Ollie's smile sparks a twinkle in her aqua eyes. "I heard that."

Enzo and Ada join the beehive of activity taking place in the kitchen. Casey is at the stove frying bacon, and Melvin is removing a bubbling breakfast casserole from the oven.

"Morning," Sheldon says, greeting them with tall round glasses of mimosas. "Charles isn't coming, but Hugh should be here any minute."

"I'm here now." Hugh barges into the kitchen, looking like hell and smelling like booze. "What's this about?"

Sheldon slaps him on the back. "I see you brought your good mood with you this morning, bro."

Hugh grunts. "I'm pressed for time. Can we get on with it?"

"Relax," Sheldon says, placing a mimosa in Hugh's hand.

As they are putting the food on the table, Ada notices Melvin discreetly slip away and head off toward the winery. They sit down with Sheldon and Ollie at opposite ends of the table and everyone else in between. Sheldon offers their family's blessing, and they pass dishes around.

"I want you to hear the news from me first," Sheldon says. "I'm taking a leave of absence from Love-Struck. Dad's phony illness didn't factor into my decision, but it has caused me to act sooner than I originally planned."

"For how long?" Casey asks, scooping casserole onto her plate.

"I'm not sure. I'll reassess the situation after the baby comes. Maybe forever."

"Are we supposed to be surprised?" Hugh asks, working on his second mimosa. "Because I saw this coming a mile away. I predicted she'd suck you in, once the two of you started playing house together."

Sheldon glares at him. "Shut up, Hugh. I don't owe you any explanations. My allegiance is to my wife and child."

"I'm considering making a change as well," Casey says. "I haven't figured out what yet, but my primary goal is to put as much distance between Daniel and me as possible."

"You can have your old job back anytime you want," Ollie volunteers.

Casey smiles at her. "Thanks. I'll keep that in mind. Problem is, I really enjoy my work at Love-Struck."

Hugh pushes his untouched plate away. "If the point of this breakfast meeting is to gang up against Dad, I don't want any part of it. I'm not condoning what he did, but he needs our support now more than ever." He gets up from the table and leaves the porch.

Silence settles over them as they listen to the sound of Hugh's truck speeding away.

"I figured he'd react like that," Sheldon says as he spears melon balls with his fork. "But I had to at least give him a chance. We can speak freely now that he's gone. Ollie and I are hoping to buy Valley View Vineyard across the street."

Casey looks up from her plate. "That's exciting. I didn't realize that property was for sale."

"It's not officially on the market," Ollie explains. "Sadly, the couple is getting a divorce. They're friends of ours and asked if we'd be interested. We made them a handsome offer. If the sale goes through, we have major plans for expansion."

"Please keep this between us for now," Sheldon says. "I'd hate for anyone else to make an offer."

Ada understands that a*nyone* is Hugh.

Sheldon turns to Ada. "What're you and Enzo doing about the wedding?"

"We discussed that before we came. We're still getting married. We're thinking a small family wedding. Just not at Love-Struck. We haven't worked out the details yet."

"I know how important getting married in the chapel is to you. You can make it a private ceremony with only Reverend Lawrence and your attendants, which I'm honored to be one of." Sheldon looks to the other end of the table at his wife. "Ollie and I would love it if you had your reception here."

"Great idea!" Casey says, crunching on a slice of bacon. "You can have an elegant sit-down dinner including the rest of the family with Luke playing in the background. His solo performances are the best."

Ollie passes the breadbasket. "Fiona will serve a dinner fit for royalty. Pun intended. And she makes the best wedding cakes ever."

Ada laughs out loud. "Did the three of you discuss this before we got here? Because you've obviously given it some thought. But I'm flattered, and it sounds lovely." She rests a hand on Enzo's arm. "What do you think?"

He covers her hand with his. "I think you're blessed to have such caring siblings. The wedding they describe is just our speed."

They divvy up tasks while they finish eating. Sheldon will speak with Daniel about using the chapel. Casey will talk to Luke about music and send out a notice to the invited guests, letting them know the bride and groom have decided to have a private family wedding. Ada will discuss flowers with Laney. And Ollie will work with Fiona to devise a proposed dinner menu.

"There is something else we need to talk about," Sheldon says over coffee. "When word of Dad's faked illness gets out, he'll lose the respect of his peers. I'll give Hugh credit for being right about one thing. Outward appearances are important for the vineyard's reputation. We need to band together against the gossipmongers. But we can't control what happens inside the family. I'm done. My relationship with Dad will never be the same." His eyes glisten. "Which breaks my heart. I'm not only losing a father, I'm losing my best friend. But I'll never be able to trust him again."

"And you can't have a relationship without trust," Ada says solemnly.

"You and I have had our differences in the past," Sheldon says to Ada. "But I'm hoping we can put the petty sibling rivalry behind us."

Ada swallows past the lump in her throat. "I'd like that. I've always respected you, Sheldon. But you were always mom's favorite, and I let my jealousy get the best of me. As for Daniel, I let him convince me to give him another chance. After the way he treated me, he didn't deserve it, and now he's out of my life for good. Even though I'm not a Love by blood, I will always think of you as my brother."

"We have the same mother, Ada. You're my half sister. And you were raised in the Love family, which makes you one of us."

Sheldon's eyes travel the table. "I'd like for the five of us to be a family. To celebrate holidays and birthdays together." He smiles down the table at his wife. "Ollie even suggested we have a standing dinner every Sunday night."

"I love that idea," Casey says, and Ada nods. "Me too."

"Charles and Hugh are always welcome in my home. But I don't owe them anything, and I won't go out of my way to be close to them. Once again, it comes down to trust. Hugh is only out for himself. As for Charles . . . who knows how he feels about anything?"

Sheldon pauses to sip his coffee. "I'm afraid Dad stands to lose more than his reputation. Marabella called me early this morning. She's terribly upset, says she can't work for Dad after what he did. I offered her a job here. She's not getting any younger, but she still has plenty of energy left. As good as she's been to our family, we owe it to her to take care of her in her old age."

"I agree." A warm feeling overcomes Ada as she remembers childhood days spent baking cookies in the kitchen with Marabella. "Your children will be lucky to know her." She stands and begins gathering plates. "I've enjoyed our meaningful talk, and I'm sorry we have to leave, but we need to get to the wine shop."

Everyone pitches in to clear the table, rinse the dishes, and put away the leftovers. Amidst hugs and kisses, Ada and Enzo bid everyone goodbye.

"What just happened?" Ada says to Enzo when they are in the car on the way back to town.

"Sheldon just appointed himself head of the anti-Daniel branch of the family."

Ada stares out the window. "Right. And now that the battle lines are drawn, I have a sinking feeling war is on the horizon."

CHAPTER 26
DANIEL

Daniel studies his reflection in the mirror as he shaves. After a sleepless night, his appearance is haggard, with dark circles under his eyes and deep lines in his forehead. He really messed up this time. It's going to take a lot of groveling to worm his way back into his children's good graces.

Dressing in khaki slacks and a golf shirt, he descends the back stairs. He anticipates the intoxicating smells of frying bacon and fresh-brewed coffee, but Marabella's not in the kitchen. He finds an envelope on the counter with his name scrawled in her tiny script. He tears open the envelope and reads the note. After decades, she's resigning from her position as the family's cook. He ran the help off. Things are worse than he thought.

Eyeing Ruthie's basket of cheddar muffins, he bites into one, but it's gone stale, and he spits it back out in the sink.

He'll go to the diner for breakfast. It'll give him a chance to assess Ruthie's anger. But when he arrives at the diner, Tanya, the head waitress tells him Ruthie has left town.

Daniel narrows his pale green eyes. "What do you mean, she left town?"

Tanya, smacking on a piece of chewing gum, says, "She called late last night. She woke me up, and I was too sleepy to comprehend much of what she was telling me. She didn't say why, but she needs to get away for a while to clear her head. She didn't know where she was going or when she'd be back. She left me in charge, because I have the most seniority, not because I have a clue how to run this place. Ruthie does everything around here. She hates delegating authority."

Daniel lowers himself to a stool at the counter. "Did she leave you in charge of her finances as well?"

"Heck no! She asked her accountant to do that. I expect she'll call today to check on things. Want me to tell her you stopped by to see her?"

"That's probably not a good idea." Daniel orders a coffee to go and leaves the diner.

He goes to Ruthie's house to search for clues of her where-abouts, only to discover his key no longer fits the locks. Which means she called an emergency locksmith late at night to change the locks before she left town. She means business. Her message is clear. She is done with Daniel Love.

His spirits plummet as he returns to the vineyard. Making amends for his deception is proving to be more difficult than he imagined.

Irritation creeps up his neck when he finds Hugh waiting for him in his office. He'll eventually get to Hugh, but right now he's more eager to speak with Sheldon and Ada.

Sitting down at his desk, Daniel says, "I have a full morning, son."

"This will only take a second. You don't owe me any explana-tions. I'm certain you had a legitimate reason to pretend like you were dying."

"The pathology department in Charlottesville mixed up my results."

Hugh frowns. "Is that what really happened?"

Daniel looks at his son as though he's an idiot. "Of course not. But that's what I'm telling people. I expect you to do the same."

"Yes, sir." Hugh squirms in his chair. "I thought you should know Sheldon is trying to turn the others against you."

Daniel tenses. "Can you be more specific?"

"He invited us all to breakfast to inform us he's taking a leave of absence from Love-Struck. Casey is considering making a change as well."

"Was Ada at this breakfast?"

"She was. But I didn't hang around long enough to hear her bashing you. They're bailing on you, Dad. But not me. You have my full support. I'm here for you, whatever you need."

Daniel notices Charles passing by in the hallway and calls out, "Charles! Can you come here please? I need a word with you."

Hugh, realizing this is his cue to leave, hurries out of his office.

Charles appears in the doorway, and Daniel motions him to Hugh's vacated chair. "We need to talk."

"What about? I have a call in a few minutes."

"Sit." Daniel motions him to a chair, and Charles eases down to the edge of the seat.

"Did you attend the breakfast meeting at Sheldon's this morning?"

Charles stares down at his lap. "He invited me, but I didn't go."

"The family is divided on how to proceed after learning of my miraculous recovery from cancer."

His attempt at making a joke falls short. Instead of laughing, Charles glares at him.

Daniel drops his smile. "I need to know whose camp you're in."

Charles casts a nervous glance at the door. "I'm not in anyone's camp. However, this might be a good time for me to do something different with my life. I've been contemplating it for a while. I'm tired of living under Hugh's shadow."

"What would you do?"

"I haven't figured that out yet. But I need to support my wife. I hope you'll allow me to stay here while I do."

Daniel works hard not to show disgust for his weak son. "Of course, Charles. Whatever it takes to make you happy." He stands and walks Charles out of his office.

When they part in the hallway, Daniel goes down to Casey's office. He waits in the doorway until she gets off the phone. She motions him in but refuses to look him in the eye, which Daniel interprets as a bad sign.

He looms over her desk. "A little bird told me you're thinking of making a change. Is that true?"

"You drove me to it," she says, scribbling something on a notepad.

"I made a mistake, Casey, and I'm sorry. I never meant to hurt anyone. Can't you give me another chance?"

She tosses her pen on the desk and sits back in her chair. "You're a self-serving, egotistical dictator. You've been jerking me around for months, playing on my emotions to get what you want. But you went too far this time, Daniel. I don't know what my mother ever saw in you. Perhaps your relationship didn't last long enough for her to see your true colors."

Her insult stings, leaving him at a loss for words. "What sort of change are you planning? I have a business to run. I'm evaluating the situation, and I need to know who I can count on."

Casey lets out a sigh. "I love my job, Daniel. I don't want to leave Love-Struck. But I need to minimize my interaction with you."

Daniel considers this good news. Over time, she'll soften toward him. "These offices are large enough for us to stay out of each other's way. Until further notice, I'll communicate with you via my assistants."

"Assuming those assistants don't resign when they find out you were fake dying."

"Ouch. That hurts," Daniel says, rubbing his arm. "I guess I deserved it."

She sweeps a hand at the door. "If you don't mind, I have work to do."

Daniel slumps his shoulders and puts on his sad face as he exits her office. Instead of returning to his own office, he leaves the building and drives over to Foxtail Farm, where a field worker directs him down to the barn.

Daniel stands in the barn's doorway, observing Sheldon as he works on a tractor. His golden boy, his best friend. They've been through so much together, and it breaks his heart to think Sheldon has turned against him.

Daniel clears his throat as he enters the barn. "Since when are you a mechanic?" he says in a joking tone.

Sheldon doesn't look up from his work. "I've developed a lot of new hobbies these past few weeks."

"Being a grease monkey doesn't suit you."

Sheldon tosses his wrench into his toolbox with a clang. "You don't know what suits me. I'm only just learning that myself. Ollie encourages me to try new things. Turns out I can do more than order people around."

"In other words, you weren't challenge enough at Love-Struck. Is that why you're taking a leave of absence?"

"Wow! News travels fast." Sheldon slams the engine cover shut and faces Daniel. "What do you want, Dad?"

"To apologize and ask for your forgiveness," Daniel says in his most sincere manner.

Sheldon hangs his head. "You made a real mess of things, Dad. You hurt a lot of people with your little charade. I'm not a crier, but I shed actual tears at the prospect of losing you."

Daniel places a hand on Sheldon's shoulder. "I am truly very sorry, son."

"Your apology is as fake as your terminal cancer diagnosis." Sheldon walks out of the barn, waiting for Daniel to follow him before sliding the door closed behind them. "Coincidentally, Ada has decided to cancel her reception at Love-Struck, but she'd still like to have the ceremony in the chapel with attendants only. No friends or family, which means you're not invited. I assume this won't be a problem for you."

"Since when are you Ada's spokesperson?"

Sheldon throws his leg over the seat of a four-wheeler. "Since you betrayed us and tore our family apart."

"You're the one tearing our family apart by making your siblings choose sides."

"Everyone was turning against you. That was your doing. I'm trying to keep us together. I already lost my father. I don't want to lose my siblings too." Sheldon starts the engine and peels off, disappearing over a hill into the vineyard.

Daniel waits until he's in his car before clicking on Ada's number. After five rings, the call goes to voice mail. He tries two more times before leaving a winded message, apologizing for his actions and begging for her forgiveness.

They'd come so far in the planning process, he can't believe Ada is canceling her dream wedding. *Their* dream wedding. And she's forbidding him from attending the ceremony. In his own chapel, no less. Obviously, he's not invited to the reception either. Where will she have it? He answers his own question. Probably at Foxtail Farm.

Out of all his children, Hugh is the only one willing to forgive Daniel. And even he has an ulterior motive. Hugh wants Daniel's title, his office, and his house. Daniel won't just turn everything over to him. His children need to fight for the privilege of running Love-Struck. May the best man, or woman, win.

CHAPTER 27
ADA

Ada is leaving the wine shop late afternoon on Saturday when her phone vibrates the console with a call from Daniel. She taps the decline button, but he calls back immediately. This time she lets it ring over to voice mail. He's been calling and texting nonstop for three days. Why can't he take the hint? She doesn't want to talk to him.

At the next stoplight, she deletes the message without listening to it. She's no sooner set the phone back down on the console when it vibrates again, and Bud's name appears on the screen. He hasn't contacted her since the grand opening, since overhearing Stuart's confession.

Snatching up the phone, she answers in a cheerful voice. "Hi, Bud."

"Hello, Ada. It's good to hear your voice. I have a surprise for you. Any chance you can drop by the farm?"

She glances at the dashboard clock. Enzo won't be home for another hour, and they have dinner reservations at Belmonte's at seven thirty. "I can spare a few minutes now if that works."

"Now is perfect," Bud says. "I'll meet you at the stables."

Ada makes a U-turn and heads out of town toward the equestrian center.

Bud greets her with a kiss on the cheek and a warm embrace. "I heard about Daniel. I don't know what to say, Ada. His behavior is unforgivable. No sane man would put his children through something like that."

"Daniel Love is the sanest man I know. Which makes what he did dangerous. I should never have let him coerce me back into his life. But I won't make that mistake again."

The lines in Bud's forehead deepen. "What my son did to you is equally unforgivable. I should've listened to you when you accused him of poisoning Glory. I had no idea Stuart was capable of something so sinful."

Ada walks over to the split rail fence and stares out at the horses grazing in the pastures. "The last thing I wanted was to come between you and Stuart. He's been an only child all his life, and I don't blame him for being upset. He shouldn't have to share his inheritance."

Bud joins her at the fence. "That's not for Stuart to decide. I didn't come from family money, Ada. I've built everything I own. When the time comes, I will choose who gets what. With that said, I admit I may have acted too hastily for everyone involved." He angles his body toward her. "I was enjoying getting to know you. I miss our morning trail rides. Do you think we can start over, no strings attached?"

Ada smiles over at him. "I would like that very much. I've missed your company as well." She turns her back on the pastures. "So, what's this big surprise?"

"It's down at the old barn. Come. I'll show you." Bud takes her by the elbow and guides her down a worn path, away from the stable.

"What is this place?" Ada asks as they approach the old red barn.

"It belonged to the original owners. When I bought the prop-erty, instead of tearing it down, I thought it'd be neat to fix it up. I found quite a few treasures in here." When they reach the barn, Bud stops walking and turns toward Ada. "I ran into

Sheldon at the diner. He informed me of your change in wedding plans. I would never dare consider walking you down the aisle in Daniel Love's chapel. However, if you allow me, I'd like to drive you from the chapel to Foxtail Farm in this." He slides open the barn doors to reveal a hunter-green, horse-drawn carriage built for two passengers and a driver. "I had it restored last year. I've been waiting for the right occasion to go for a test drive."

Ada's golden-brown eyes double in size. "This is seriously cool. I absolutely love it. Do you think Glory will pull us?"

"We'll certainly try. If not, I'm sure we can find a horse that will."

Ada throws her arms around Bud's neck. "This is outstanding. Thank you!" She circles the buggy, admiring the shiny exterior and running her hand across the soft leather bench seat. "We'll have Laney create a garland of greens and flowers for the back."

"I'm glad you approve," Bud says, beaming from ear to ear.

"Wait until I tell Enzo. And speaking of Enzo." She consults her watch. "I should get home. We have dinner reservations. Are you free for a trail ride in the morning?"

Bud bends slightly at the waist. "I'm at your beck and call, milady."

They iron out the details for their trail ride as he walks her back to the stables. When they reach her car, Ada turns to him, kissing his cheek. "Thank you for your incredibly thoughtful gesture. I can't wait to ride in the carriage on my wedding day."

"And I can't wait to drive you. We'll hook Glory up one day soon and go for a practice run."

Ada waves at him as she drives off. At the farm's entrance, she pauses to check her phone. She's received ten missed calls from Daniel during the brief twenty minutes she was out of the car. Clearly, he's not giving up. And she needs to set him straight, not over the phone but in person. Besides, there's something she wants from The Nest. She's been thinking a lot lately about her mother's portrait above the mantel in the living room. She'd like nothing more than to have the painting hanging in their new house.

Ada sends a text to Enzo, asking him to push their dinner reservations back thirty minutes before continuing onto the highway. As she passes through the Love-Struck entrance columns, she encounters a long line of cars leaving the vineyard from an afternoon wedding reception.

She parks in front of The Nest and rings the doorbell. Daniel's voice calls out from within. "Coming!" When he swings open the door, confusion crosses his face. "You're not Bruce."

"Nope. Not Bruce." Ada flashes her phone at him. "You've been blowing up my phone for three days. You obviously have something to say to me, so I figured I'd give you a chance to say it in person. Get it all off your chest, as this will be the last time we talk. Ever again."

"Oh, sweetheart. You don't mean that," he says, reaching for her arm.

Ada glares at him, warning him not to touch her.

"I never meant to hurt anyone. My intentions were good. But my judgement was flawed. When I decided to fake my illness, I was still under the effects of anesthesia from my surgery."

"So now you're blaming the anesthesia," Ada says, tossing her hands up in exasperation. "You told us you were dying, Daniel. You intentionally caused your children enormous sorrow. Do you even understand how sick that is?"

"I'm not the cold-hearted monster you make me out to be. I wasn't thinking. I was desperate to have you back in my life." He steps out of the doorway. "Come inside, Ada. Let's talk. We can work this out."

Unhappy memories from her childhood greet her in the hallway, preventing her from going any farther. "There's nothing left of our relationship to work out. It's over, Daniel. We're finished."

His face crumples. "But you're getting married in a few weeks. The wedding plans are already made."

Ada holds her head high, despite her pounding heart. "The

wedding plans have been unmade. We have notified the guests. I'm getting married in the chapel with only my attendants and Reverend Lawrence. You are not invited."

"But it's *my* chapel," Daniel says, sounding like a little boy fighting over a treasured toy.

Ada's brow arches toward her hairline. "So it's *your* chapel now? Never mind you're always going on about how the property belongs to the Love *family*. Last I heard from you, I'm still a part of that family. Or are you going to pull the blood card again?"

"I explained all that. Genetics don't matter. I was upset with your mother, and I took it out on you."

"More excuses. You raised me as your daughter, a Love child the same as Sheldon and Hugh and Charles. You can't change my name, and you can't erase the past. This vineyard is as much a part of me as my skin." Her anger growing, Ada pauses to catch her breath before continuing. "As a child, I used to hide in the chapel when you and Mom argued. And when she died, I spent a lot of time there mourning her. I have a right to get married there."

"I'm not stopping you from getting married in the chapel, Ada. I'm just saying I should be there."

"And I'm saying you're not invited."

Daniel lets out a loud sigh. "Fine! I won't attend, if that's what you really want."

"Thank you. And there's one other thing I want." Ada marches across the hall into the living room. She drags an ottoman over to the fireplace, kicks off her suede driving loafers, and climbs on top of it.

"What're you doing?" Daniel asks, watching her ease the portrait off its hook.

"What does it look like I'm doing?" Under the bulkiness of the portrait, she carefully steps down and slips her shoes back on. "I'm giving my mother's portrait a new home. She should be somewhere happy, far away from the man who never loved her and made her life miserable."

The color drains from Daniel's face as he grips the back of a chair.

"What's the matter, Daniel? Don't you feel well? Or are you faking again?" Ada carries the portrait out of the living room and wrestles it through the front door.

Daniel runs out of the house after her. "Don't go, Ada! I'll cancel my plans with Bruce. Or better yet, you can help us sample our new varietal. Afterward, you and I will have dinner together. We can go to the club."

Ignoring him, Ada carefully stores the portrait in the back seat of her car and gets behind the wheel.

"Please don't shut me out of your life. I can't live without you, Ada. You've always been my favorite."

"You have a funny way of showing it." She slams the door in his face and speeds off.

Ada waits for the rush of adrenaline to hit. After months of turmoil, she finally broke her bond with Daniel. But instead of feeling elated, she's empty inside. Her sense of loss is profound. The life she's always known at Love-Struck Vineyard is over. And the man who is more a father to her than Bud Malone will ever be is lost to her forever.

CHAPTER 28
LANEY

Laney returns to the shop after the wedding at Love-Struck. She takes her time unloading the Suburban and resetting her workroom for Monday. With her daughters once again at sleepovers, the only thing waiting for her at home is another argument with Hugh followed by a lonely night in the guest room staring at her four cream-colored walls. She misses Bruce and their late-night phone calls more than she ever imagined possible.

Laney sits down at the worktable with a pen and pad to make notes from the messages left on her shop phone throughout the day. She has plenty of orders to keep her busy next week. Business is thriving and she's ready to hire an assistant, but it must be the right person. They will be working long hours together. She wants someone she can confide in. Someone who will be a friend.

She locks up and stops in at Delilah's for prepared meals for their dinner. She chooses a spinach salad with grilled shrimp for herself and meatloaf and mashed potatoes for Hugh. She experiences a flash of annoyance as she imagines Hugh waiting at home for her to fix him dinner. She returns the meatloaf to the shelf. Let him starve. He needs to learn he can't take her for granted.

Laney has become increasingly bolder with her insults in

recent days, which has resulted in a worsening of their arguments. She's pushing him to the edge, and he's holding on by a thread. When that thread snaps, he'll come after her and she'll be ready. She paid Diana the first month's rent for the upstairs apartment and brought over some clothes and necessities should she and the girls need to flee from home.

As usual, Hugh is waiting for her at the kitchen table. "Where have you been?" He clinks the ice cubes in his empty glass before refilling it with bourbon.

"I told you. I guess you didn't listen. I had an afternoon wedding today. When I left the vineyard, I took my supplies back to the shop." She pours a glass of wine and sits down with her salad, placing her phone screen side up on the table in case one of the girls sends her a text.

Hugh eyes her salad. "Where's *my* dinner?"

Laney shrugs. "I didn't get anything for you. I assumed you'd be eating at the club after golf."

"I came home right after golf so I could spend time with you. I'm trying to be nice here, Laney. You're not making it very easy."

She lowers her gaze as she pours dressing on her salad. "If you wanted to do something nice, you could've planned dinner for me. A grilled steak would've hit the spot after my long day at work. When's the last time you cooked on the grill? Oh, wait! I forgot. I'm responsible for grilling. Like I'm responsible for every-thing else around here."

"You're the wife. It's your *job* to feed your family."

"Things have changed. Being a floral designer is now my primary *job*." Laney delivers this jab with a smile. She finds it makes him madder.

"I guess I'll make myself a sandwich." He leaves the table and strides over to the kitchen, where he places slices of ham and cheese between two pieces of bread. Returning to the table, he says, "The truth is, I don't enjoy grilling."

Stabbing a forkful of salad, Laney says, "What do you enjoy

besides golf? Certainly not hiking or rafting or cycling like the girls and me."

Her phone dances on the table with an incoming call. She freezes with her fork in midair when Bruce Wheeler's name appears on the screen.

Hugh looks from the phone to Laney, his eyes flickering with anger. "Why is he calling you?"

Laney's blood runs cold. "I have no idea. I haven't spoken to him in days."

"You lying bitch. You're still sleeping with him." Hugh kicks his chair out of the way as he dives across the table at her. Salad flies in the air and her wine glass crashes to the floor. The impact of his body sends them toppling backward with arms and legs flailing.

When they hit the ground, Laney sees stars. As her head clears, she remembers the handgun in her purse on the counter. She worms her way from beneath his weight, but as she's clambering to her feet, he yanks her back down, straddling her with her arms pinned against her sides. He punches her face repeatedly with both fists, violent blows to her eyes and cheeks and mouth. She wraps her legs around his torso, and with all the energy she can muster, she wrestles him off of her.

She's back on her feet and running down the hallway. She senses him on her heels, but she's afraid to look back. She's nearing the front door when a heavy object strikes her in the back of the head. Her knees weaken, and she collapses to the floor.

When she regains consciousness, Hugh is pressing something to the back of her head with one hand and helping her sit up with the other.

"Get up, Laney. Dad had a medical emergency. I'm not sober enough to drive. You need to take me to the hospital."

The pain is unbearable, and she can't think straight. What happened to her head? Then she remembers the fight. She shoves him off of her. "Give me a minute."

"Here." Hugh takes her hand and presses it against the cloth on her head. "Hold this against your wound. You're bleeding all over the rug."

She grips a console table as she pulls herself to her feet. She has no business driving in this condition, but the hospital is the safest place for her. Fortunately, it's only a couple of miles away.

Laney leans against the wall for support as she makes her way to the kitchen.

"What're you doing?" Hugh asks. "We need to go."

"I'm getting my purse. I can't drive without my license."

"I'll get it for you," he says, brushing past her down the hallway.

She calls after him. "No! Wait!" She can't let him feel the weight of the gun in her bag. "I need a minute to compose myself."

"Whatever." He retraces his steps down the hall. "I'll wait for you in the car. But hurry. Dad needs me."

Laney makes her way past the overturned furniture and broken glass to the kitchen. She hides the handgun behind boxes of baking supplies in an upper cabinet, replaces the bloody cloth on her head with a clean one, and recovers her phone from the debris on the floor. Despite having a cracked screen, the phone still appears to work.

She's exiting the house when she notices her heavy antique brass candlestick on the floor near where she fell. Beside the candlestick is a pool of blood. She glimpses her reflection in the mirror over the console table. She's a character from a zombie apocalypse movie with swollen eyes, a busted lip, and hair caked with blood.

On the way to the hospital, Laney drives with one hand on the steering wheel and the other the cloth on her head. "How did you find out about your father?"

"Sheldon called."

Laney doesn't remember Sheldon calling. How long was she unconscious?

"Well? What did he say?"

"Only that Bruce found Dad unconscious when he went to The Nest to share a sample of a new varietal."

"So that's why Bruce was calling me," Laney says in a matter-of-fact tone.

They ride the rest of the way in silence. When they arrive at the hospital, she parks the car and turns off the engine.

"We'll tell everyone you fell down the stairs." Hugh's tone is conspiratorial, as though he expects her to go along with him.

Laney doesn't argue. She has every intention of telling the truth.

Bruce and Sheldon are waiting near the entrance to the crowded emergency room.

Anger burns in Bruce's eyes when he sees Laney's face. "Did he do this to you?"

"Yes," Laney says, her voice almost a whisper.

Bruce goes after Hugh with fists flying. Sheldon attempts to break them up while Laney summons a security guard for help.

The security guard grabs the men by the collars, holding them at arm's length to separate them. "What's the matter with you two? This is a hospital. There are people suffering here."

"Look what this man, her husband, did to her face." Bruce squirms to free himself, but the guard easily holds him in place.

The guard studies Laney's face. "Whoa. You need medical attention."

Laney locks eyes with her husband. "I want to file a report with the police first."

"We'll get to that." The guard looks back and forth between Bruce and Hugh. "I'm gonna turn you two loose. Anymore funny stuff, and you're going to jail."

Freed from the guard's grip, Bruce rushes to Laney's side. "You're deathly pale. Are you gonna pass out?"

"Maybe. I feel lightheaded," she says and collapses against him.

An orderly with a wheelchair appears. As he's wheeling her

off, Laney's eyes meet Hugh's and he sags in resignation. *At long last, he realizes our marriage is over.*

Laney welcomes Bruce's presence in the treatment room. He knows all the right questions to ask the nurse about her head wound. Does Laney have a concussion? Will the doctor use stitches or staples to close the wound? Will they give her a CT scan to determine if her skull is fractured?

After the nurse inserts an IV, another nurse whisks her away again for the scan. When she returns to her treatment room, Bruce is speaking with a young female police officer who is waiting to take her statement. Laney describes her troubled marriage and the events that took place earlier tonight at their home.

"Can you prove your husband did this to you?" Officer Sims asks.

Bruce lets out an irritated huff. "Isn't her word enough?"

"Evidence would seal the deal," Sims says.

"My house is a crime scene." Laney's eyes dart around the room. "Where's my purse? I'll give you the keys, and you can see for yourself."

Bruce retrieves her purse from the locker at the foot of the bed.

Laney digs through her bag for her keys and hands them to Sims. "The kitchen is a war zone, and on the floor near the front door, you'll find the candlestick my husband used to clobber me over the head."

"Yes, ma'am. I'll be back in a while." The officer departs the treatment room, leaving Laney and Bruce alone for the first time.

"I need to text my divorce attorney," Laney says, her thumbs flying across the cracked phone screen. Her message reads: *I'm at the hospital. I now have evidence of physical abuse. I'd like to file for divorce right away.*

When Laney looks up from her phone, Bruce is watching her with a tender expression. She smiles softly at him. "I would love nothing more than for you to hold me right now, but now is not the right time for us to come out of the closet about our relationship. I want to be sensitive to the Love family. They are going through a lot."

Bruce moves to the edge of his chair. "I agree wholeheartedly. Does that mean we can't be friends?"

"We can be friends. I'm glad you're here."

"Me too. And I'm not going anywhere. I promise not to pressure you. We'll decide together if and when the time is right."

Laney reaches for his hand. "You know how I feel about you, Bruce. It's not *if*. It will definitely be *when*. Tell me what happened to Daniel. Is he pretending again, or did he really have a medical emergency?"

"Appears to be the real deal. Daniel and I made a date to sample the red blend I've been working on. When I arrived at The Nest, I found him lying unresponsive on the ground in the driveway. I called the rescue squad. The paramedics are pretty sure he suffered a massive stroke."

CHAPTER 29
ADA

Ada is struggling to remove her mother's portrait from the back seat of her car when a gust of wind from an approaching cold front nearly rips it out of her hands. Coming to her rescue, Enzo takes the painting and carries it inside to the fireplace mantel, where he props it in front of his framed NBA basketball championship poster.

Ada grabs his arm. "What're you doing? You can't cover up your favorite basketball poster."

He laughs. "I don't remember ever claiming it as my favorite poster. I don't even like basketball that much. I just bought it because it looked good in this room." He stands back to admire the portrait. "Your mother was a striking woman."

"She was movie star glamorous. When I was a little girl, I remember her descending the main staircase on her way out for the evening, dressed just like this in a black velvet gown with her dark chocolate hair coiled in a chignon and a choker of pearls around her neck."

"How did you get the painting?" Enzo asks. "Did you burglarize The Nest?"

"I didn't have to. I took it off the wall while Daniel watched."

Enzo casts her a sidelong glance. "You actually went to see

Daniel?"

"He wouldn't stop calling me, and I had some things I needed to say to him. I figured he'd listen better if I said them in person. I'll tell you about it over dinner."

"About dinner . . ." Enzo pulls Ada in for a half hug. "What say we stay home tonight? We can open a bottle of red wine and build our first fire of the season. We can snuggle up while you tell me more about the famous Lila Love."

Ada sinks into him. "I like this idea, but what will we eat? I'm getting hungry."

"What about chicken nachos? I have a hankering for Mexican."

"Sold. I'll cancel the dinner reservations, pour the wine, and turn on the gas logs while you make the nachos."

"I'm on it," Enzo says, kissing the top of her head before disappearing into the kitchen.

Fifteen minutes later, they are cozied up on the sofa with glasses of an Argentinian Malbec wine and a platter of chicken nachos on the coffee table in front of them. "Are you sure you don't mind having Mom's portrait in our home?"

"Mind? I'm thrilled. She was extremely elegant." Enzo points a tortilla chip at the painting. "People might mistake her as one of my royal ancestors."

"Haha," Ada says, shoving him with her shoulder. "Mom had striking features. But part of her elegance was the way she carried herself."

"I can think of a handful of places to hang it in our new home. Above the mantel in the living room would be the obvious choice. Or we could put it above the sideboard in the dining room."

Ada jerks her head toward him. "What sideboard?"

A smile tugs at the corner of Enzo's lips. "The antique one I bought at an auction a couple of weeks ago. I hope you don't mind. I couldn't resist."

"Why would I mind? I grew up with antiques. I like a mixture of old and new."

"One would never know based on your ultra-contemporary

apartment," Enzo says, digging his chip into the cheesy topping.

"My tastes have changed since I met you. Speaking of which, don't forget we're meeting with the decorator on Monday to pick out paint colors."

He groans. "I think I'll sit this one out. I trust your judgement. As long as you don't paint everything white."

"We'll have plenty of color in our home. Just nothing as dramatic as this," she says about his navy walls.

Enzo looks suddenly at his phone. "Why is Sheldon calling me?" He accepts the call. "Sheldon! What's up, man?"

Ada can't hear Sheldon's end of the conversation, but Enzo's concerned expression indicates something is wrong.

"We're on our way," Enzo says and ends the call.

"Where are we going?" Ada asks, her heart pounding against her rib cage. "Did something happen?"

Enzo gets up, takes her wine from her, and pulls her to her feet. "Daniel was taken to the hospital by ambulance about an hour ago."

"What for? Another phony medical condition intended to elicit sympathy from his children?"

"This sounds serious, Ada. Bruce found Daniel unconscious in the driveway at The Nest."

Ada's brow pinches. "In his driveway? But I was just there. He was fine when I left." Or was he? She was so anxious to leave she didn't bother looking in the rearview mirror. Did something happen to him after she drove away? Could she have had a psychotic episode and run him over with her car, and is now blocking what happened from her memory?

The possibility she might have hurt Daniel festers in her mind while she takes the nacho tray to the kitchen and grabs a jacket from the bedroom. When she expresses her concern to Enzo on the way to the hospital in his truck, he laughs at her. "Don't be ridiculous, Ada. You're not capable of running anyone over in your car. Even if you were in a psychotic state. Anyway, the doctors think it was a stroke."

"A stroke? That's not good." She turns toward the window, staring out at the passing lights. "Now that I think about it, Dad seemed a little shaky while I was there. Why did Sheldon call you and not me?"

"Because he didn't think you'd come to the hospital unless I made you."

"He's probably right."

When they arrive, they follow Sheldon's instructions and take the elevator to the second-floor ICU waiting room where the rest of her family is huddled in one corner—Hugh, Sheldon and Ollie, Charles and Hazel, Casey and Luke, her sexy saxophone player.

"What's the word?" Ada asks the group.

"None yet," Sheldon says. "We're still waiting for the doctor to give us an update."

Hazel pulls Ada aside. "Laney is being treated in the emergency room downstairs. Hugh attacked her earlier tonight, before they got the call about Daniel. Someone needs to check on her. Charles won't let me."

Ada shakes her head, unsure if she heard Hazel correctly. "What do you mean, he won't *let* you?"

"He says I shouldn't get involved, that our loyalty is to Hugh, and that they probably just had a petty squabble."

"Squabbles don't typically land people in the emergency room, Hazel."

"I realize that. But Charles is upset about Daniel, and I don't want to make him mad. Will you go check on her?"

"Of course." Ada turns toward Sheldon, who is standing with Enzo behind her. "Did you know about Laney?"

Sheldon nods grimly. "I saw her when they got here. Her injuries aren't life threatening, but she's pretty banged up."

"What happened to Laney?" Enzo asks.

"Hugh beat her up." Ada stands on her tiptoes to kiss Enzo's cheek. "I'm going down to the emergency room to check on her. Call me if the doctor shows up."

The attendant standing guard in the emergency room refuses

to let Ada see Laney. "But I'm her sister-in-law," Ada argues. She flashes her driver's license at the sour-faced nurse. "See, we have the same last name. Love."

"That means nothing. There are lots of Loves in this town."

Ada glares at her. "Can't you at least tell her I'm asking to see her?"

"I guess." The disgruntled nurse disappears through the double doors and returns a minute later. "She's in the third room on the right."

Ada bursts through the double doors and hurries down the hall. She's curious to see Bruce emerging from Laney's treatment room. She remembers how Laney softened when Ada mentioned Bruce at the grand opening and wonders again if something is going on between them. Is that why Hugh attacked her? Did he discover they were having an affair?

Regardless, she'll use this opportunity to ask about Daniel. "When you found Daniel in the driveway, did you notice any trauma to his body?"

"Only some scratches on one cheek where he scraped the steps when he fell. The paramedics seemed certain he had a stroke. Has there been any word about his condition?"

Ada shakes her head. "We're still waiting for the doctor."

Bruce stuffs his hands in his pockets. "I'm going to the cafeteria for some coffee. Can I get some for you?"

"I'm fine. But thanks." Ada watches him walk down the hall before entering Laney's examining room. She's taken aback by the sight of her sister-in-law's battered face. "Oh, honey. I'm so sorry. Does it hurt much?"

Laney touches her fingers to her temple. "I feel like an elephant is stomping on my brain."

"Tell me about your injuries."

"Besides what you see on my face, I have five staples in the back of my head and a mild concussion."

Ada sits down in the chair next to the bed. "Has the abuse been going on long?"

Laney lowers her gaze. "The verbal abuse has. But tonight is the first time he hit me. I've been sleeping in the guest room for the past year."

"I suspected you were having problems. I wish you'd told me."

"I didn't feel comfortable. He's your brother."

Ada's lip curls in disgust. "He's a monster. Will you press charges?"

Sorrow overcomes Laney's battered face. "Not as long as he agrees to a divorce and promises to stay away from me."

"I consider you family, Laney. I'm here for you, if you need anything at all."

Laney winces when she tries to smile, her hand flying to her busted lip. "That means a lot. Thanks."

Ada settles back in her chair. "I saw Bruce out in the hall. Is there something going on between you two?"

Laney's eyes well. "We're just friends. He's been helping me through a difficult time. That's not to say I don't have feelings for him. But I have no intention of acting on those feelings until I've sorted out my life."

"You're a good person, Laney. I hope you one day find happiness," Ada says, handing Laney the box of tissues from the table beside the bed.

Snatching a tissue from the box, Laney wipes her eyes and blows her nose. "How is Daniel? Has there been any word about his condition?"

"Not yet." As the words leave Ada's mouth, Enzo's picture appears on her phone's screen. She accepts the call, but before she can say hello, he blurts, "Ada! The doctor's here. Hurry."

Ada jumps to her feet. "I've gotta run, Laney. The doctor's updating the family now." She kisses the tips of her fingers and presses them gently to Laney's cheek. "Hang in there. I'll check on you in a couple of days."

Ada runs down the hallway, out into the waiting room, and past the line of people waiting for the elevator. Locating the stairwell, she takes the stairs two at a time on the way up to the second floor. Her family is gathered around the doctor, who is speaking technical terms in a serious tone.

Ada wedges between Enzo and Sheldon. "What'd I miss?" she whispers to Enzo.

"Nothing I understand," Enzo says, placing a reassuring hand on her shoulder.

The doctor, an attractive man in his fifties, rattles on in medical jargon about the different types of strokes.

Hugh finally snaps, "Get on with it, Doc. Describe our father's condition in layman's terms."

The doctor glowers at Hugh. "Your father is stable, but not out of the woods yet. We won't know what physical impairments the stroke has caused until he regains consciousness. Since the stroke affected the left side of his brain, I expect him to have some paralysis on the right side with the potential for memory loss and difficulty speaking. Without question, he's facing a long and difficult recovery ahead. You might as well go home. There's nothing more you can do for him tonight."

"When can we see him?" Hugh asks.

"If you're willing to wait, you can probably see him tonight—although he's unconscious and won't know you're here." The doctor tucks his iPad under his arm and leaves the waiting room.

Hugh drops to his chair. "Y'all can go home. I'll stay with Dad."

Ada leans down and whispers to Hugh, "Because you no longer have a home to go to, you wife beater."

Ada and Enzo walk with the others out of the hospital. Charles and Hazel peel off toward their car while everyone else congregates in the middle of the dark parking lot.

"What're we supposed to do now?" Casey asks.

Sheldon pulls his wife close. "Ollie can attest to how much of a basket case I've been these past few weeks when I thought Dad was dying from colon cancer. I can't go through that again. For the sake of my pregnant wife, I have to emotionally detach for now."

Ada shivers, chilled by the approaching cold front. "I hate seeing anyone suffer. Including Daniel. But his stroke doesn't change how I feel about him. Not after all he's put me through these past few months."

Casey's eyes shine. "I agree. I've been a wreck since Daniel came into my life. It's best if I distance myself from him and focus on my work." She looks at Luke, and he thumbs a tear off her cheek.

Ada's heart warms. The two make a cute couple. She's thrilled her new friend has someone to help her sort out her life post-Daniel.

Sheldon says, "Since the three of us are out of the picture, we can let Hugh deal with Dad's recovery. He's moving into The Nest for the time being, anyway, while they determine the conditions of the divorce. Focusing on Dad will be good for him. Not that I really care what is good for Hugh."

"Me either. Not after what he did to Laney." Ada offers the group a sad smile. "I don't want to lose touch with you guys, especially now that we're growing closer."

Ollie's aqua eyes brighten. "This is as good a time as any to start our Sunday suppers. Everyone is invited to dinner at Foxtail tomorrow night," she says, and they part with hugs and words of encouragement.

On the way to the truck, Ada says to Enzo, "There was a time when I relished revenge. But I feel like the most insensitive person on the planet right now. There is no pleasure in ganging up against Daniel."

"Don't think of it as revenge, Ada. Think of it as self-preservation."

Ada pauses a beat as she considers his suggestion. "You're right, Enzo. That's exactly what Daniel would do if the situation were reversed."

CHAPTER 30
LANEY

The loud ringing of Laney's cell phone startles her out of a deep sleep on Sunday morning. Expecting one of the girls, she sits bolt upright to accept the call, but falls back against the pillows at the sound of Hugh's voice. "Where are you?"

"I'm at home. The doctor released me around three this morning."

"How'd you get home?" Hugh asks, suspicious.

"Bruce drove me."

"Whatever," Hugh says in a disgusted tone. "I thought you'd want to know Dad has regained consciousness. He can't speak, and he's paralyzed on his right side."

"I'm sorry to hear that, Hugh." Her tone is genuine. She *is* sorry for Daniel. But not sorry enough to forgive Hugh for what he did to her.

"I'm moving into The Nest where I can oversee his home care and recovery when he's released from the hospital. I'll be by later this morning to get my stuff."

Laney sits up again. "I don't want you in the house. I'll pack up your belongings and leave everything in the garage. You can pick them up after three this afternoon."

"Are we really going down the divorce road, Laney?"

"I can't believe you would ask me that after what you did to me last night. Goodbye, Hugh. My divorce attorney will be in touch." Tossing the phone on the bed beside her, she draws her knees to her chest as she looks around the room. She's spent her last night in the guest room. Today, she reclaims her life.

Laney calls the alarm company to change the code on their security system and locates a locksmith willing to work on Sunday. While he changes all the locks on the house, she cleans up the kitchen and scrubs the bloodstain from the wooden floor near the front door.

The girls arrive home from their sleepovers around lunchtime. At the sight of Laney's face, Ella lets out a loud sob, and Grace beams red with anger. "I assume Dad did this to you." Without waiting for Laney to respond, she adds, "I hope you kicked him out."

Laney, unable to speak for fear of crying, nods.

"It's about time," Grace says, and darts up the stairs.

Ella throws her arms around Laney. "Oh, Mama! Are you okay? Does it hurt much?"

Laney strokes her daughter's hair. "I'm fine, sweetheart, aside from a little headache."

"I've been so scared. I know he's my dad, but I hope he never comes back."

They hold each other for a long time until Ella finally pulls away. "I've gotta ton of homework. I'd better get started."

Mother and daughter walk up the stairs together. When Ella disappears into her room, Laney goes to the attic for empty boxes.

For the next several hours, she folds Hugh's clothes in boxes and stores them along with his golf gear in the garage. She gives the master bedroom a thorough cleaning before moving her things over from the guest bedroom. She's missed her bedroom with its adjacent marble bath, built-in shelves and drawers, and sweeping view of her backyard. She can hardly wait to slip beneath the clean crisp sheets in her king-size bed later tonight.

For dinner, Laney orders pizza and a Greek salad from their favorite Italian restaurant. They sit down at the table for the first time as a threesome. While Hugh's chair is noticeably empty, the conversation is livelier than it's been in months as the girls talk about their innocent shenanigans at their sleepovers.

Turning serious, Grace asks, "Where is Dad living now?"

"At The Nest for the time being." Laney explains about their grandfather's medical emergency, which leads to a long discussion about strokes and subsequent lengthy recoveries.

Grace's face is pinched when she asks, "Will you have to share custody with Dad? Because I never want to see him again."

"I'll have to ask the divorce attorney, honey. I'm not sure how the process works. Since you girls are older, I would think you'd be allowed to express your wishes to the judge." Laney takes a sip of her sweet tea. "I realize you're upset with your father right now. And understandably so after the past few months. He needs help. Hopefully, the divorce will prompt him to get it. For now, you can be comforted in knowing he's never coming back here to live."

This appears to appease them, and the mood at the table once again lightens. They have a long road of healing ahead of them, but at least tonight was a start.

———

Laney finds Hazel waiting at the shop's back door when she arrives at nine thirty on Monday morning. "What're you doing here?"

Hazel studies her bruised face, but she doesn't comment. "I thought you might need some help this week. I know little about flowers, but I can take phone orders and greet customers. With your . . ."—she touches a finger to her cheek—"I figured you might not want to see people."

Laney laughs. "You're so right." She unlocks the door and motions Hazel inside.

Hazel, needing little instruction, gets right to work sweeping the showroom, wiping down the countertops, and answering the phone. Laney creates bouquets to sell on the sidewalk and prepares for the week's upcoming events.

Around noon, Laney hands Hazel a twenty-dollar bill and sends her next door to Delilah's for sandwiches. They prop open the swinging door to watch for customers while they eat at the workroom table.

"When did you first realize your marriage was over?" Hazel asks.

Something in Hazel's tone makes Laney wonder if Hazel and Charles are having marital problems. She sets her sandwich down and wipes her mouth. "On a hot summer night in July of last year. I told Hugh I was thinking about getting a job, and he went ballistic."

Hazel removes a slice of unripe tomato from her sandwich. "But you already had a job doing wedding flowers."

"Hugh never considered that a job. And I was hoping for something more time-consuming. Anyway, a horrible fight ensued. Our problems were too serious to handle on our own, but when I suggested we see a marriage counselor, he adamantly refused. I moved into the guest bedroom that night. I've been sleeping there ever since."

"Wow," Hazel says, her doe eyes wide.

Laney can tell something important is on Hazel's mind, and she waits for her to say more. When she remains silent, Laney pries, "You seem troubled. Is there something you want to talk about?"

Hazel stares down at her sandwich, her honey-colored hair hanging in her face. "I'm bored out of my mind. I left the accounting firm to start a family. That obviously hasn't happened."

"Have you given up trying to have children?" Laney asks, sipping her sweet tea.

Hazel shrugs. "I haven't given up. But Charles doesn't believe in fertility treatments. I'm not sure he even wants children anymore. He's not the same person I married."

"How so?" Laney asks, taking a bite of her chicken salad croissant.

"He used to be fun. Now he's always in a sullen mood. That sounds petty. I shouldn't complain. Charles is an excellent provider, and he's reliable. He comes home every night for dinner at six on the dot."

Laney remembers Hugh saying Charles often leaves the vineyard for lunch and never returns. She wonders where he spends his afternoons. "Do you two argue?"

"Actually, it's the opposite. We hardly ever talk. We still do outdoorsy stuff every weekend, like hiking and rafting, but we don't connect anymore. There's no romance. It takes two to make a baby."

Laney reaches for her hand. "Oh, honey, I'm so sorry."

Fat tears appear in her enormous eyes and slide down her cheeks. "I'll be thirty-nine in November. I thought about divorcing him, but by the time I find a new husband, my child-bearing years will be over. If I want to have children, Charles is my best shot."

"I understand your logic." Laney squeezes her hand before letting go. "Have you considered going back to work, to take your mind off of things at home?"

Hazel nods as she wipes her eyes and nose with a napkin. "But I don't want to go back to accounting. I'd like to do something fun. Like what you're doing here. And you're right. It feels good to get out of the house. You don't have to pay me, but I can continue working here this week while your face is healing."

Laney sits up straight. "Are you kidding? You're a godsend. Of course I'm paying you. I've been thinking of hiring a full-time assistant. Let's see how it goes. If you like the work, we can talk more at the end of the week."

Hazel's face brightens. "That'd be great. Tell me more about your business."

While they finish eating, Laney tells her about the weddings and holiday parties she's booked for the coming months.

"Gosh, that sounds like a lot."

Laney laughs. "I know! Just talking about it overwhelms me." Getting to her feet, she gathers up their sandwich wrappers. "Are you worried how Charles will react to you working for his brother's soon-to-be ex-wife?"

Hazel hesitates before responding. "For the first time in a long time, I don't care how Charles feels. I've devoted myself to a dead-end marriage. I need to save myself before it's too late." She stands to face Laney. "But I'm scared. Charles and I have been married for ten years. I don't know how to live life without him."

"Of course you're scared. But you're stronger than you think." Laney pulls her in for a hug. "A friend gave me the courage I needed to stand up to Hugh. If you'll let me, I'd like to do the same for you."

"A friend is exactly what I need right now." The tension leaves Hazel's body as she crumples into Laney's arms. They embrace for several long minutes until Hazel pulls away. "Will you show me how to do an arrangement?"

Laney smiles. "You bet. It's easier than you think."

Hazel knows more about flowers than she let on, and she has a natural knack for putting together an aesthetically designed arrangement. They slip into easy conversation as they work, and they learn more about each other in one afternoon than the ten years they've been sisters-in-law.

Hazel has already gone for the day, and Laney is locking the front door when she notices Diana, elegant in a black jumpsuit, coming up the sidewalk. She steps outside to greet her.

"Why that rotten bastard," Diana says in response to Laney's bruised face. "I had a gut feeling I should stop in to check on you today. I hope you kicked his sorry ass to the curb."

"I did." Laney smiles, touching her finger to her busted lip when it stings. "But I think the feeling in your gut was for another reason. I was going to reach out to you. Is the building still for sale? And how much are you asking for it?"

Diana tells Laney the asking price. "But make me your best offer," she says, sinking her long nails into Laney's arm. "I just sold my house in Lovely, and I'm motivated to sell this building too."

Laney turns to face the building. "I will talk to the bank first thing in the morning."

"The building is a sound investment. But why would you need the apartment if your husband is out of the house?"

Laney looks up at the second-floor windows. "I've grown fond of the apartment. I may use the living room as my office. I hope Hugh will cooperate with the divorce. In case he doesn't, knowing I have a safe place gives me peace of mind."

"That makes sense. And truthfully, the rent on the apartment and the shop combined are probably less than a mortgage."

"True." Laney walks with Diana to the end of the sidewalk. "I'll be in touch once I figure out my finances."

"I'm not in a hurry, Laney. I want you to have the building, and I'm willing to wait until you can make that happen."

Laney, her voice tight with emotion, croaks out, "You're too good to me, Diana. I can never repay your kindness."

"Seeing you thrive is all the thanks I need." Diana places a gentle hand on Laney's cheek. "You're on your way. Go chase your dreams, pretty lady."

As Diana lowers her hand from her face, Laney kisses the inside of her wrist. "I will."

Laney watches Diana's tall, lean figure disappear into a crowd of people on the sidewalk before finishing locking up. She's getting in her car when, on a whim, she darts up the stairs to the apartment. She throws open all four windows in the living room, letting the crisp autumn air flow through. Why does this place have such a powerful hold on her? Is it because she feels safe tucked up here, away from the world? Or is it because it might be hers one day? Her very own piece of real estate she bought with money she earned herself.

She roams about the living room, imagining her office space. The room is big enough for her to section off a corner for her desk and filing cabinets, leaving plenty of space for the sitting area.

The sound of loud banging on the shop door downstairs draws her to the window. She hollers down to Bruce, "Yoo-hoo. I'm here. Come on up."

She hears footfalls on the stairs, and he appears in the doorway with two cups of gelato. "It's pistachio, your favorite," he says, holding a cup out to her. "I would've brought you flowers but . . ."

She laughs, taking the cup. "I have all the flowers I need. You didn't have to bring me anything. But I'm glad you did."

"I've been thinking about you all day. How're you holding up?"

"Better than expected. But I'm tired. Let's sit down." In club chairs opposite each other, Laney tells him about Hazel's surprise appearance this morning, her visit from Diana at closing time, and the possibility of buying the building. "My business is doing better than I ever imagined. Besides, if my budget gets tight, I can always rent the apartment. The previous owner's husband was planning to rent it through Airbnb."

"That's an excellent option as well. As fast as this town is growing, you can't go wrong."

"How're things at the vineyard?"

"Not great, honestly. Hugh's on a rampage, making everyone miserable. He pulled me aside today. He's convinced you and I are having an affair. He told me he'd fire me if we weren't so close to launching the varietals. I'll drag it out as long as I can, but once the new wines are launched, I know he'll force me to resign."

Laney's face falls. "Where will you go?"

"In order to continue my career, I'd have to move back to California. Since your divorce agreement will likely prevent you from leaving the state with your girls, and since I'm not leaving you, I may take a job at the hardware store."

Laney bursts out laughing. "Admit it. You have a burning desire to sell hammers and nails for a living."

"Maybe," he says, shoveling a spoonful of gelato into his mouth.

"Hugh won't fire you. He wouldn't dare go against his father's wishes. And Daniel loves you."

"But Daniel is in a bad way right now. He may never fully recover. We'll have to wait and hope for the best."

Laney digs her spoon into her gelato. "How are the other Love children handling Hugh's wrath?"

"Sheldon has taken a leave of absence until after the baby comes. I haven't seen Charles. He didn't come in to work today. And Hugh's bossiness is making Casey a nervous wreck."

"Sounds like war is brewing at Love-Struck. I'm glad I'm not involved." She takes their empty gelato cups and walks them to the trash can in the kitchen. When she returns to the living room, Bruce is standing at the window.

"Penny for your thoughts," she says, standing beside him.

He turns toward her. "I know it's inappropriate for me to kiss you. But is it asking too much for me to hold you?"

"Not at all. You've been a true friend to me, Bruce. I would never have survived these past weeks without you."

He extends his arms, and she walks into them. She rests her head on his chest, listening to his heartbeat. And what a lovely sound it is.

CHAPTER 31
DANIEL

Daniel's brain is dense with the fog of confusion. Rare and brief moments of clarity provide glimpses of his bleak new reality. He can neither move his right-side limbs nor speak. He is now imprisoned within his own body.

Over time, the faces of the hospital staff hurrying in and out of his room become familiar. He develops favorites among the nurses. The pretty blonde whose soft touch and floral scent remind him of Ruthie. And the heavyset woman with caramel skin and a voice as sweet as honey who reads to him from the Bible when he can't sleep during the night.

Hugh is the only one of his children who visits Daniel. To his credit, he never misses a day. But sometimes Daniel wishes he would leave. Hugh goes on at nauseating length, criticizing his siblings' ineptness. Sheldon has formally taken a leave of absence. Charles never shows up for work. And Casey is too afraid of her own shadow to be of any use to him. While his criticism infuriates Daniel, in this condition, he's powerless to take up for his other children.

"I'm divorcing Laney," Hugh admits during a late-afternoon visit. "For the girls' sake, I'm letting her stay in the house. I've moved back into The Nest for the time being. I can help you get back on your feet when you come home." He squirms in his chair. "You won't believe it, Dad. She's having an affair with Bruce. Totally blindsided me. I thought we had the perfect marriage." He scrunches up his face and makes crying noises, but no tears spill from Hugh's eyes.

Daniel has a hard time believing this about Bruce or Laney. He never understood what Laney saw in his oldest son. Then again, Hugh was somewhat likable when they married. And he could be charming when he tried. Something happened to him over the years to turn him into an ill-tempered, vindictive jerk.

Hugh stands, as though preparing to leave. "Under the circumstances, Dad, I'm not sure I can continue to work with Bruce. Once we launch the new varietals, I'm going to let him go."

Daniel groans his protest, but Hugh either doesn't hear him or ignores him as he exits the room.

A few days later, Hugh tells Daniel about the changes he's making to Daniel's renovation plans. "I've given the new tasting room a different look. Your modern rustic vibe isn't cutting it for me. We need something trendy and edgy."

Heat flushes through Daniel's body. He doesn't want an edgy tasting room.

Hugh sits back in his chair, crossing his legs. "And the terrace expansion is all wrong. If our goal is attracting a younger crowd, we should incorporate an outdoor bar with a wide-screen television. A sports bar is exactly what this town needs, a hangout for locals to watch football games in the fall and the Masters Tournament in the spring."

Daniel's heart races and his blood pressure alarm sounds. Since when is attracting the younger crowd a priority? He'd envisioned a casually elegant restaurant with farm-to-table cuisine where sophisticated patrons can drink wine and enjoy the beauty of their surroundings.

A nurse rushes in to reset the alarm. She wags a finger at Hugh. "If you're going to upset the patient, I'll have to ask you to leave."

Hugh holds up his hands in surrender. "Sorry! No more business talk. I promise."

As soon as Daniel shows the slightest signs of improvement, the doctors transfer him to a rehabilitation facility over in Hope Springs, and Hugh's visits drop off to every few days.

The rehabilitation facility is worse than anything Daniel has ever experienced. To describe the staff as negligent is an understatement. Hours pass between visits from nurses. Three excruciatingly long days go by before an orderly wheels him down for his first physical therapy session. The process is painful, and the therapist incompetent, and Daniel returns to his room feeling utterly hopeless and helpless.

That night, he reaches the depths of despair. He can't tell anyone how he's feeling, anymore than he can get up from his bed and walk out of this wretched place. He's ready for the afterlife, even if that means a fiery encounter with the devil.

The next day, when Hugh arrives to find his gown soiled and bed soaked with urine, he immediately places a call to Daniel's concierge doctor. "Dr. Harmon, this is Hugh Love. I need your help. We have to get Dad out of this rehabilitation facility," he says and explains about the unacceptable conditions.

Hugh is sitting close enough for Daniel to hear Jason's voice over the phone. "I'm sorry to hear that, Hugh. I will report your experiences to the medical board. Unfortunately, your next closest choice for a rehabilitation facility is in Charlottesville."

"That won't work. I'm taking Dad home. Today."

Jason doesn't hesitate. "I'll contact his neurologist and make arrangements for his release."

Daniel closes his eyes and says a prayer of thanks.

Jason continues, "I can order an ambulance to transport him back to Lovely, but you'll need to organize nurses and therapists to care for him at home. As soon as we hang up, I'll text you a link to a list of potential providers."

"Thank you, Dr. Harmon. I owe you one."

Hugh crosses the room to the door and begins barking orders

at the nurses out in the hall. Within minutes, Daniel is wearing a clean gown and lying on fresh sheets.

For the next two hours, Hugh places numerous phone calls as he plans for Daniel's at-home care. At five o'clock, the ambulance arrives to transport him to Love-Struck. An hour later, he is resting in his own bed at The Nest.

Hugh lowers himself to the edge of the mattress. "Don't get too comfortable up here. This is only temporary until we can set up a hospital bed in your study. You can't navigate the stairs in your condition. Being on the first floor will make it easier for everyone."

Daniel is too grateful to argue. He'd sleep in the stable if it meant staying at the vineyard.

They hear footfalls on the steps, and Claude appears in the doorway. If the nursing assistant is angry with Daniel for lying about his cancer diagnosis, he doesn't show it.

Shooing Hugh out of the room, Claude gives Daniel a thorough sponge bath, dresses him in his favorite paisley silk pajamas, and tucks his comfy covers in around him.

Daniel falls into a deep sleep, and when he wakes the following morning, Marabella is setting a breakfast tray down on his nightstand. She scowls at him. "I may be back, but I'm still mad at you. You'd better not lie to me again, Mr. Love. You hear me? I mean ever."

Daniel dips his head in a slight nod, the left side of his mouth turned upward.

"I loved working for Miss Ollie and Mister Sheldon. But with the baby on the way, they need someone younger than me." She chuckles. "I'm too old to care for an infant. I've raised my children. And yours too."

She sits down beside him on the bed and gently spoons oatmeal into his mouth. "Claude and I are gonna take care of you. When we're done, you'll be as good as new. But you gotta listen to us, do as we tell you," she says as she continues to feed him.

Daniel moans in pleasure. The oatmeal is the best food he's

had since before his stroke. He'll do anything to keep Marabella in his kitchen.

A delivery van from a home medical equipment company arrives midmorning with a hospital bed and various other paraphernalia geared toward invalids.

Daniel thrives under Marabella's and Claude's strict supervision and excessive pampering. Within a few days, he's sitting up on his own in a wheelchair, although his speech and the use of his hand is slow to return. His mind is clearer every day, but with too much spare time to think, he obsesses about his future.

Daniel's neurologist is pleased with his progress when he goes for his checkup appointment the last Wednesday in October. "If you keep up the hard work, you can expect a full recovery."

Daniel suspects his time as head of the vineyard has come to an end. He will need to determine his successor.

Hugh talks increasingly about the changes he's making at the vineyard, changes that don't sit well with Daniel. While he's forever beholden to his son for saving him from the godawful rehabilitation facility, he's not willing to turn over his life's work to someone who doesn't share the same vision for the vineyard. Daniel would like to maintain the grace and serenity of the property while Hugh aims to turn it into Disney World.

Casey would be a good choice, if only she weren't so young and new to the industry. Charles is out of the picture. He doesn't have enough sense to come in out of the rain. Sheldon would be Daniel's choice. He'd love to see a merger between Love-Struck and Foxtail, but he doesn't think Ollie would ever go along with it.

An idea takes seed in Daniel's brain. Why not make his children an offer they can't refuse and see who rises to the occasion with the most dignity?

CHAPTER 32
ADA

The late October afternoon sun streams through the windows, casting an ethereal glow over the chapel as Ada and Enzo exchange wedding vows. Warmth floods Ada. Her mother's presence is strong. Lila is smiling down on them from above.

Reverend Lawrence pronounces them husband and wife, and Enzo kisses his bride. He scoops Ada off her feet and carries her down the aisle and out the front of the chapel. Bud, a dashing figure in tails and top hat, is waiting with the photographer beside the carriage. Bud helps Ada into her fake fur shrug and offers her a hand as she climbs into the carriage.

Enzo pops the cork on a bottle of Dom Perignon and hands out glasses to his bride, their attendants, and Bud. After posing for dozens of photographs, Bud taps Glory gently on her rear with his whip, and she clomps off down the drive.

Enzo places an arm around Ada, drawing her in close. "How does it feel to be a princess?"

She cuts her eyes at him. "Don't I get a coronation ceremony?"

He laughs out loud. "Nope. You're officially a princess, Princess Ada of Puglia."

Ada sticks her lower lip out in a pout. "Bummer. I wanted the crown."

When they pass The Nest, Ada's heart sinks at the sight of Daniel in his wheelchair in the driveway in front of the house. Even from the distance, she can see he's crying. This was to be their special day, the fairy-tale wedding they've dreamed about since she was his little princess.

Ada forces thoughts of Daniel from her mind. He brought this on himself, and she refuses to let him ruin her wedding day.

At the end of the driveway, instead of taking a right toward Foxtail Farm, Bud guides Glory to the left toward town.

"Where are we going?" Ada calls out to him.

Over his shoulder, Bud says, "I thought we'd make a quick trip down Magnolia Avenue."

"Oh goody," Ada says, clapping her hands like a delighted child.

Tourists and locals cheer and call out congratulations as they parade down the town's Main Street.

"Now, I feel like a princess," Ada says with head held high as she waves back at the crowd.

Ada is moved by the sight of her friends and loved ones waiting for them in front of The Foxhole when they arrive. Sheldon and Ollie. Casey and Luke with his saxophone. Hazel and Charles. Laney and her girls.

Ada and Enzo dismount the carriage as white rose petals shower down around them. Bud tips his top hat at her. "Have a wonderful evening, lovebirds. I'll be back around nine to drive you over to Hope Springs."

Ada blows him a kiss. "Are you sure you can't come back for dinner?" She's asked him several times to join them for dinner, but he insists she have this time alone with her Love siblings.

He offers her a soft smile. "I'm positive. I need to get the carriage back to the farm before dark," he says and lifts his reins.

Ada watches them disappear up the driveway before joining the party, already in progress. The setting is magical with globe lights strung in a crisscross pattern across the terrace and a rectangular table set with creamy candles and bouquets of white flowers. Luke plays soft jazz while servers bear trays of hors d'oeuvres and champagne flutes.

Ada makes the rounds, speaking to each of her guests.

"You look amazing," Laney says. "Your gown is to die for. And it's so you."

"Thank you." Ada studies her sister-in-law's face. "The bruises are gone."

"Finally! I'm grateful to see my own face in the mirror instead of that battered old hag." Laney turns serious. "I didn't know if Hugh would be here."

"I didn't invite him. Having both of you would be awkward, and I picked you. I will always consider you family, Laney. Ella and Grace are my nieces. I hope the divorce doesn't come between us."

Laney smiles. "It won't if we don't let it. Besides, we'll be seeing a lot of each other now that we're shop neighbors."

"By the way, you did an amazing job with my flowers. How're things going with Laney's Bouquets?"

Laney's face lights up. "Business is booming. Hazel is working for me full-time. She's a whiz at arranging flowers. Actually, she's a whiz at every task she undertakes."

Ada's gaze shifts to Charles and Hazel who are standing off to themselves, looking miserable. "Except making Charles happy."

"Whatever Charles's problem is has nothing to do with Hazel. As far as I'm concerned, she's an angel."

"No one has ever held Charles accountable for anything," Ada says. "He's always been Hugh's shadow. When something happens with Charles, we look to Hugh to deal with it."

"Unfortunately, we're all guilty of giving Hugh too much control," Laney says and excuses herself to check on her girls.

Sheldon and Casey appear on either side of Ada. Casey hooks an arm around Ada's neck and bumps her hip. "Look at us, girl-friend! We've come a long way in a few short months."

Ada laughs out loud. "Are you kidding me? Those months have been the longest of my life. Speaking of which, I saw Daniel today when we drove past The Nest after the ceremony. I must be getting soft, because I felt kinda sorry for him."

"I've softened some too," Sheldon says. "I've missed him these past few weeks. I can't imagine not having him in my life. But I have no clue how to start over."

"You can start by going to see him," Casey says. "I went for the first time yesterday. He looks bad. He's lost a lot of weight and his hair has gone white. But he appears to be making progress. He even said a couple of words."

Sheldon hangs his head. "I feel guilty for letting Hugh handle Dad's care. While Hugh is not my favorite person, it's unfair for him to bear the burden alone."

Casey lowers her gaze. "It's not my place to say this, but if you ask me, Hugh is milking the situation. He's taken charge of the vineyard, making decisions Daniel wouldn't approve of." She clears her throat. "That's why I went to see Daniel. I've tried to reason with Hugh, but I'm in over my head. But Daniel didn't seem surprised. I think he already knows what's going on."

"How could you tell?" Ada asks.

"He gave me a lop-sided smile and patted my hand in a reassuring way. The twinkle in his eyes let me know he's not finished at Love-Struck Vineyards. He may be down, but Daniel Love is definitely not out."

Sheldon grins. "Knowing Dad, he's scheming up a way to make a dramatic comeback."

Ollie joins their group. "Fiona says it's time to eat. The food looks and smells scrumptious."

"I'm sure it'll be delicious," Ada says.

"Let's round up the posse," Sheldon says and finger-whistles for everyone's attention.

The guests gather around him for a heartfelt blessing before migrating to the table. Ada and Enzo are seated with their backs to the cafe, looking out over the vineyard. Sheldon is to Ada's right and Casey to Enzo's left. Charles and Hazel are at the heads with the others in between on the opposite side.

They've no sooner begun eating their autumn salads when Hugh staggers around the corner of the cafe from the parking lot.

"What's up?" he says, his words slurred. His bloodshot eyes travel the table. "I see the gang's all here. Sheldon, the golden boy. Casey, the bastard child. Charles, the mute." His gaze lands on Laney. "I'm hurt, Ada. I can't believe you invited my soon-to-be ex to your wedding and not me." He digs his thumb into his chest. "I thought I was your favorite brother. Or are you too good for me now that you've married an Italian prince."

Ada stands to face him. "For Enzo's sake, I'm working hard to be a better person. You should try it sometime, Hugh. Living the clean life has its rewards."

Hugh lets out a grunt. "So, you're a righteous woman now. We'll see how far your new code of ethics gets you in life."

Catching sight of his daughters, Hugh staggers around the table. He stands behind Ella and Grace, stroking their long auburn hair. "I've missed you, girls. Your bitch of a mother refuses to let me see you."

Laney jumps to her feet. "Stop it, Hugh! You're scaring them."

He positions himself in boxing stance with feet apart and fists raised. When Laney flinches, he lets out a maniacal laugh. "Look at the fraidy cat. You're not nearly so brave without your police protection. Drop the charges already. I'm not going to hurt you again."

"The Commonwealth of Virginia is prosecuting you, not me."

Sheldon comes around the table and takes Hugh by the arm. "You're way out of line, bro. You need to leave."

Hugh jerks his arm free. "Get your hands off me. I have something to say before I go." He hiccups. "You-holier-than-thou assholes should be ashamed of yourselves for not visiting Dad. I've convinced him to make some big changes at the vineyard. I'll be rewarded for my loyalty, and all of you will be left out."

"Good for you. Now go." Sheldon's arm shoots out with finger pointed toward the parking lot.

Hugh gives Sheldon the middle finger, and on unsteady legs, he retraces his steps around the corner of the cafe.

"Go after him," Ollie cries to Sheldon. "Before he kills himself."

No one says it, but Ada suspects they're all thinking the world would be a better place without him.

Sheldon remains glued to the spot, as though deciding whether to go after Hugh. "I guess I should," he says finally and takes off at a jog. He hasn't gotten far when a loud crash echoes throughout the night. Chairs push back and feet hit the ground running. When they reach the front of the cafe, off in the distance near Ollie's farmhouse, the glow from the full moon illuminates the mangled metal of Hugh's sports car wrapped around a tree.

Guilt punches Ada in the gut. Only moments ago, she was thinking the world would be a better place without him. And now he's gone. A collective gasp pierces the silence as a shadowy figure appears from the smoking wreckage. Hugh stumbles toward them, then turns back in the direction of the road.

Laney pulls her crying daughters close. "He seems disoriented. Should we call for help?"

"Not yet," Sheldon says, his eyes on his brother. "If we involve the police, they'll arrest Hugh for drunk driving, and the story will be all over local news. I'll go check on him. If he's okay, I'll drive him home. If not, I'll take him to the hospital."

"I'm going with you." Ada gathers up the hem of her dress and steps in line beside Sheldon.

Casey and Enzo join them, and the foursome marches up the driveway toward the wreckage.

"Are you sure we shouldn't call the police?" Enzo whispers to Ada. "The man is a menace."

"Maybe so. But he's a Love. And we protect our own." She loops her arm through his. "Welcome to the family, Enzo. Another day, another family drama."

. . .

War breaks out among the Love sibling when Daniel announces a campaign to choose his successor in *Love and War,* the next episode of The Virginia Vineyard series. Click HERE for links.

If you're loving the Virginia Vineyard series, you might enjoy my Palmetto Island and Hope Springs series as well. Watch the trailers and learn more on my website.

And . . . to find out about my new and upcoming books, be sure to sign up for my newsletter.

Sweeney Sisters Series

Saturdays at Sweeney's

Tangle of Strings

Boots and Bedlam

Lowcountry Stranger

Her Sister's Shoes

Magnolia Series

Beyond the Garden

Magnolia Nights

Scottie's Adventures

Breaking the Story

Merry Mary

ACKNOWLEDGMENTS

I'm grateful for many people who helped make this novel possible. Foremost, to my editor, Patricia Peters, for her patience and advice and for making my work stronger without changing my voice. And to my cover designer, Damon and his team @ Damonza.com for their creative genius. A great big heartfelt thank-you to my trusted team of beta readers who are always available to read a manuscript, discuss plot issues, or help with cover selection. And special thanks to my publicist, Kate Rock, for all the many things you do to manage my social media so effectively.

I am blessed to have many supportive people in my life who offer the encouragement I need to continue the pursuit of my writing career. Love and thanks to my family—my mother, Joanne; my husband, Ted; and my amazing kiddos, Cameron and Ned.

Most of all, I'm grateful to my wonderful readers for their love of women's fiction. I love hearing from you. Feel free to shoot me an email at ashleyhfarley@gmail.com or stop by my website at ashleyfarley.com for more information about my characters and upcoming releases. Don't forget to sign up for my newsletter. Your subscription will grant you exclusive content, sneak previews, and special giveaways.

ABOUT THE AUTHOR

Ashley Farley writes books about women for women. Her characters are mothers, daughters, sisters, and wives facing real-life issues. Her bestselling Sweeney Sisters series has touched the lives of many.

Ashley is a wife and mother of two young adult children. While she's lived in Richmond, Virginia, for the past twenty-one years, a piece of her heart remains in the salty marshes of the South Carolina Lowcountry, where she still calls home. Through the eyes of her characters, she captures the moss-draped trees, delectable cuisine, and kindhearted folk with lazy drawls that make the area so unique.

Ashley loves to hear from her readers. Visit Ashley's website @ ashleyfarley.com

Get free exclusive content by signing up for her newsletter @ ashleyfarley.com/newsletter-signup/